THE POE CODEC

MICHAEL CRANDELL

THE POE CODEC

MICHAEL CRANDELL

A CAVE HOLLOW PRESS BOOK
WARRENSBURG, MISSOURI 2016

Cave Hollow Press™

for Stephanie, Jordan, and Lauren . . .

TABLE OF CONTENTS

Few persons can be made to believe that it is not quite an easy thing to invent a method of secret writing which shall baffle investigation. Yet it may be roundly asserted that human ingenuity cannot concoct a cipher which human ingenuity cannot resolve.

—Edgar Allan Poe
Secret Writing

codec /ˈkəʊˌdɛk/ *noun*

1. *(electronics) a set of equipment that encodes an analogue speech or video signal into digital form for transmission purposes and at the receiving end decodes the digital signal into a form close to its original*

Word Origin: from co(de) + dec(ode)
dictionary.reference.com

Fact and Fiction

Fact: Poe did ask Rufus Griswold to compile his works after his death. Ironically, Poe made this request, even though the two often bordered on being each other's enemies.

Fiction: None of the letters alluded to in the novel were ever written.

Fact: Dr. John Carter was a real person and was Poe's friend and physician.

Fiction: The Indiana Constitution of 1816 is stored in the Indiana State Archives in Indianapolis, not in Friedman University (which is fictitious).

Fact: Poe was highly interested in secret codes and encryption.

Fact: New Harmony, Indiana was an attempt at an American intellectual, utopian community. Scholars and experts in various fields came to live in the community in the 1830s.

Fiction: There is no record that Poe was invited to New Harmony by Robert Owen or had any ambition to live there.

Fact: The Working Men's Institute is an actual museum, archive, and library in New Harmony. It was founded by William MacClure in 1838.

Fact: The "punch card" loom (actually called the Jacquard Loom) is a real machine and is considered to foreshadow the first computer.

Fact: The Analytical Engine, designed by Charles Babbage in 1834, is considered to be the first multi-function computer.

Fiction: No parts of the Analytical Engine exist in the Working Men's Institute in New Harmony, nor does the Jacquard Loom.

Fiction: No known code is embedded in Poe's "The Raven" or in any of his other works.

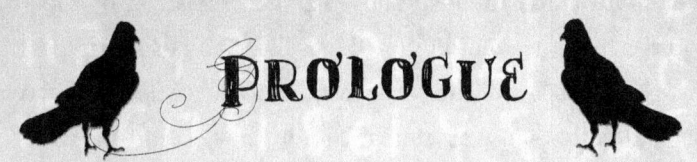

PROLOGUE

She knows.

Though she is too weak to cough, her breathing is light, raspy. She no longer tastes the salty blood seeping from her lungs, through her burning throat, and onto the burlap rags next to her head. She is numb, weightless, as if floating in a warm lake. Still, even now, with the few admirers who've come to pay last respects near her bedside, she summons what dignity she can, thanking with her eyes those changing the bloody rags and placing wet cloths on her forehead.

This isn't how to die.

Less than a year ago, she was part of the Richmond social elite, laughing at the bad jokes of the affluent over thin glasses of imported champagne, engaging in trivial small talk at get-togethers requesting her presence, despite her profession. In 1813 Virginia, acting was a career reserved mainly for the destitute and lower classes, if one strove to make more of it than a mere hobby. But Eliza Poe was the exception. She transcended the stage, entrancing the audience with her beauty—with her eyes— *becoming* the role rather than merely acting it. Her talent earned her a kind of status, carrying her from an unknown to a celebrity relatively quickly, and her popularity continued to grow.

Even after David left.

She knew from the beginning he wouldn't stay, but she loved him regardless. He too was an actor, but a free spirit, a nomad who would never survive stability, a home, a family. When she became pregnant shortly after the wedding, Eliza had the sliver of hope that they could make a normal life for themselves, as normal as possible for married actors. And later the next year when she was carrying their second child, she was almost certain they would make it "'til death us do part." But when she told David of their third, he simply stared out the hotel window, then said he would be back in a minute and walked out the door.

And never came back.

Working the theater circuit along the eastern coastline, traveling from city to city, and raising three children—alone—endeared her even more to her audience, which was why they continued to visit her.

Even now.

She motions for Mrs. Merriweather, the wife of a tobacco merchant and a wealthy admirer, to come to the bedside.

"I hate to inconvenience you," Eliza says in a whisper, "but could I ask you to grant me a great favor? I'm afraid, however, that I might not be able to return it."

"Mrs. Poe, ask of me the world, and I'll bring it here this very hour," Mrs. Merriweather says, taking her hand.

"It's my children. They'll have no family. Could you place a message in the paper asking my friends to look after my babies? My babies . . . "

"Bring them in," the doctor says to Mrs. Merriweather; feeling Eliza's pulse, he places her hand at her side, his face telling the few in the room that time is short.

The room empties as the Poe children surround the bed, the amount of blood shocking the older two, but not nearly as badly as Eddie, the youngest.

"Little Eddie," Eliza says to the dark-haired boy, not much older than three. It's all right. It's all right."

The little boy stares at the red rags scattered around the bedside.

He begins to tremble, only slightly at first, but as the horror envelops him, his entire body begins to shake. He has seen the few times his mother coughed up a small spot or two of blood from what he has heard doctors call *consumption*, which of course means nothing to him beyond the fact that it makes his momma lie in bed, sometimes for days, coughing, and crying. But this is different. He has never seen so much of it—the bright red—on the covers, on his mother's nightgown, on the pillow, on the pile of rags in the corner. His mother's life, everywhere. He feels his stomach tighten, followed by the urge to vomit.

"Eddie, come here. I want to give you something."

The boy, doesn't—can't—move. He is paralyzed by the sight of the blood. *Momma's blood*. He looks at his mother, who despite the pain and the knowledge that she will not see another sunrise, still compels a smile, and when he sees her—the last face he sees countless nights before slipping into sleep, the face which plays the silly games that only they understand—he is hesitant at first, but slowly creeps closer to the bedside.

"Eddie, honey. Listen to Momma. Do you hear me, sweetheart?" Eliza whispers to the little boy. "I'll be going to heaven in a bit. But don't you worry. You'll be getting a new momma."

The boy only stares at her with large dark watering eyes, his lower lip curling into his mouth.

"I know, my little Raven, I know, but you need to be very brave, you hear? Someone's going to take good care of you. Hold out your hand. Would you do that for me?"

He places his small hand palm up on the bed next to her side.

"I want you to have something. Will you keep it for me?"

The boy nods.

Eliza raises her hand from under the blanket and places a small silver oval into the boy's soft, pale hand, a miniature locket.

"Now look here, Eddie. When you push this little clasp, it opens. See inside there? What do you see?" she says, her voice a forced rasp.

"I see you, Momma."

Inside is Eliza's miniature clothed in a white dress with a large bowed bonnet, suggestive of a halo encircling her head. A slight smile adorns her mouth, evocative of the *Mona Lisa*. Etched on the inside of the locket's cover is a row of apparently random marks:

"That's right. See? I'll always be with you. You keep this with you, and I'll be with you. Oh, my little Raven. My little Eddie. I love you so . . ."

She tries to say more, but she can only whisper unintelligible words, her eyes fixed on the little boy's until, shortly, the sparkle in hers fades, followed by a slow, soft exhale.

But little Edgar Poe didn't understand.

Until later.

THE POE CODEC

Letter to Samuel Williams from Rufus Griswold
May, 1849

Samuel,

    I hope this letter finds you in the best of health. I will admit that it is most convenient having a physician friend such as yourself. If you would only charge half as much for your services!

    I must tell you that I received the most interesting (and should I say comical?) letter this past Wednesday, from the most unusual person. I have told you before of the conflict between E. Poe and myself, of how he constantly berates my work, as well as that of nearly all others who work with the written word. The "Comanche of Literature" wrote me in an attempt to reconcile our years of literary warfare. He wishes to make amends, and has even gone so far as to suggest that we engage in a partnership, quite possibly in the form of editing an anthology of the Great American authors.

    I laughed aloud upon reading this. He and I will never foster a friendship as I find it most impossible to learn the ways of the southern white-trash charlatan. How can he expect to mend a decade of ill-abuses, slanders, and malice with a mere stroke of the quill? As I have often said before–he is a madman–as insane as his characters. Or more so.

    I have contrived the most ingenious plan to have the last word, yes, even the last laugh. He has, in his arrogance and ignorance, asked me to serve as his literary executor after his death, a request even more preposterous than the two of us writing together! After I wiped away my tears of laughter, the most amazing idea entered my brain. I would indeed serve as his literary executor, and the world would know of the _real_ Mr. E.A. Poe! How better to avenge his relentless criticism than to ensure that the world remembers him only as a footnote?

There is power in rumor. Many of the literary audience question his talent, even so far as his sanity. Alas! Why not confirm the speculations? What if I paint such a horrendous portrait of the so-called artist, create such a foul taste in his admirers' mouths, that his reputation, his legacy, lies buried in some forgotten tomb, decaying?

But my luck is tarnished as I am sure he will yet out-live me, despite his poor health. He is a Southerner, and since Virginian folk do not easily die, I am convinced that I will yet see my grave before him.

Give my warmest regards to Katherine. I will be in New York, if time is merciful, by the end of the month. I will call on you then.

Your Friend,

Rufus Griswold

PART I:
THE PO'E CO'DEC

XSZKGVI 1

"So what do we do with it?"

"Good question."

It was just a crusty brown letter scribbled in that old style of writing with the loopy 'g's and 'y's, but it wasn't so much the age of the letter—dated September of 1849—that got Brett and Jordan's attention, as it was how they found it.

The boys knew it was trespassing (and possibly breaking and entering) when they slipped through the partially-open basement window of the empty building that used to be Hemington's Bookstore, but the temptation was too great. The diversion was too alluring.

Brett found every excuse he could to be anywhere but home, a small brick house on Woodlawn Avenue, usually vacant anyway. His father, Jeff Kerchoff, was an associate professor of Anthropology at nearby Friedman University, a small private college on the south side of Indianapolis. Although his position was tenured and somewhat secure, he had yet to publish any of his work, a failure keeping him from any advancement in pay or position. To show his department chair and dean that he was doing everything he could to produce scholarship, he arrived at his office early and left long after the night classes dismissed. He needed the recognition. And he and Brett needed the money. Badly.

The collection agency managing their medical expenses was gracious in agreeing not to pursue legal action, considering the circumstances of their debt. Brett's mother, Amanda, had died nearly six years earlier from Acute Myeloid Leukemia, and despite her brief hospitalization, money to pay for her medical expenses was always a problem — but never an issue, as his father neither complained nor even mentioned it. Yet Brett knew. They were always just one statement away from going under.

Which was why an empty house with no dad was becoming just fine with him.

And why he needed Jordan all the more.

Just beyond the shadow of the Lucas Oil Stadium in the Indianapolis Fountain Square Cultural District, Hemington's had been a landmark on the Southside since the store's opening in the late 1920s, specializing in offering rare antique books, as well as being one of the first bookstores in the nation to sell gourmet coffee. Its brick façade was in no way unique; visitors unfamiliar with the area usually had to ask directions to find it. Hemington's had had its niche for several decades, but as bookstores nationwide gradually became franchised and eventually web-based, its shelf life had expired. No longer able to compete with larger outlets offering cheaper prices, the modest store could only offer specialty coffee and something to read.

And when the owners turned the deadbolt on the entrance doors for the last time and handed the keys to the auction company, no one in the area really seemed to notice.

Or really care.

Coffee shops and bookstores in Indianapolis are anything but a scarcity.

But the old building was replete with limitless history, and both Jordan and Brett were sure it was replete with limitless wealth. The answer to all their problems.

The basement resembled a low-ceilinged underground parking garage; the open spaces between the large brick pillars that formed the building's foundation had once provided expansive storage space for old files, old inventory, and old echoes of an older time. Now it offered the boys new, unmapped terrain to conquer.

The frosted-glass windows near the ceiling illuminated the cobwebs while the boys' phone flashlights animated the shadows.

Nearly every human being alive, no matter what epoch in history they've lived, has walked through an old building and wondered what secrets were tucked away inside the walls, or what treasures were buried in the cellar's dirt floor. Such structures foster rampant fantasies of noticing a glint of misplaced light within a small crack in a wall, prying it open, and finding a burlap bag of gold coins, or a stack of Confederate money, or some other long-forgotten relic worth millions. They had no idea what they were looking for, but Brett and Jordan knew that when they found it, it would make them both millionaires.

The fantasy of the discovered treasure. The very motivation that enticed Egyptian tomb raiders to steal their Pharaoh's gold from the Pyramids. What kept the miners tunneling inside mountains, inhaling potential catastrophe with every breath or panning the creeks to find specks that tantalized them, taunted them, to pursue the quest for the motherlode that would bestow on them infinite fortune. The malady they called "The Fever" and "The Bug."

Jordan picked up a book from the floor. Several pages were missing, as well as the back cover.

"What is it?" Brett asked, shining his light towards Jordan.

"Just a torn up book."

"Let me see."

Brett held the remains of the book in his hands and smiled.

Curious George Learns the Alphabet. His first favorite series. He turned the few pages that still clung to the broken binding. He remembered the Thursday public library visits with his mother, leaving with the stack of thin books, each one a guarantee of time nestled with her on the couch, as he pretended to mispronounce the words so she would wrestle with him in mock frustration, then they would put their blond heads together, look into the eyes that mirrored their own, and play the I-love-you-I-love-you-more-no-I-love-you-more game until she kissed his nose and ended the game by saying, "but I loved you first."

She herself had gradually become pictures in a box stuffed in the hall closet, his memories of her fading like the colors of the pages he held, which was why he kept one of her small senior pictures folded and tucked between the case and the back of his phone. He rarely looked at it, but he knew it was always with him. And that would have to be enough.

Brett rubbed his finger along the edge of the book cover.

"You care if I keep it?" he asked Jordan.

"What do I care? It's not mine," Jordan replied. "Probably not worth anything anyway."

To Jordan, books were the tools of life you were forced to use because you had no other choice, like using a toilet plunger. You didn't really enjoy the experience while using them, but you didn't want to deal with the mess if you didn't. He would rather *do* life than read about it, even one like his.

Jordan lived with his grandmother a few houses from Brett's on Woodlawn Avenue, and the two could never really remember when they first met; it just seemed they were always best friends. Jordan was left with his grandparents when his mother moved to Seattle shortly after he was born. She had gotten pregnant by her boyfriend, a college student home for the summer of her junior year, and when she told him the news, he said he would go back to school and finish the next semester, and then they would get married. She never saw him again.

After she graduated from high school and had Jordan, she lived briefly with her parents. Then one day, she was gone. Her parents eventually heard from her, though she gave no explanation or apology for her sudden disappearance, only told them she was living in Seattle. And that was the last they heard from her.

Jordan's grandfather died of cancer within a few months of Brett's mother's death, and these common tragedies in their lives only solidified the brother-like bond they shared but would never dare mention. They didn't have to. They knew.

Jordan's grandfather had driven a truck for a delivery company, and the small pension he had accumulated shriveled up when the company went bankrupt not long after he retired, leaving Jordan's grandmother the challenge of seeing how far a monthly check could go. Jordan understood, and never asked for money, never complained about not having enough. He loved her too much to even consider it, which was why he talked Brett into climbing through the bookstore basement window. Not to steal. To discover. To find their fortune.

They quickly discovered, however, that any item granting anyone fame and fortune had already been sold at auction or scavenged by junk dealers acute in the economics of the salvage resale industry. And Jordan was quickly becoming bored anyway, which meant things would quickly become interesting.

Brett suppressed a horrendous fear of insects; anything crawling or flying spawned ice in his stomach. Since second grade, it had been a source of endless entertainment for classmates to walk behind him in the hallway going to lunch or recess and lightly place a piece of string or a strand of yarn on the top of his ear or the back of his neck and watch him convulse and jerk to free himself from whatever lethal organism he believed had every intention of opening his skull with razor teeth or acidic tentacles and devouring the gray matter in his brain. Brett fell for it every time and would attack the perpetrator with a rage-fueled vengeance, although he would never hold a grudge, at least not for long. He was granted a sympathy reprieve from the badgering in fifth grade after he failed to outrun a disoriented wasp that had flown through the open classroom window, impelling him to run face-first into an open locker door and having his chin rejoined with eight stitches. But the shelf life of sympathy is fairly short in fifth grade.

And had completely expired by now, the eighth.

Jordan found a small piece of plastic wire insulation on the floor and carefully positioned it across the back of Brett's neck.

Instantly, Brett screamed, frantically brushing at his neck, jerking, convulsing, spinning in panicked circles.

"Get it off! Get it off me now!"

Jordan fell against a wood-paneled column, hitting his head as he threw it back laughing, and coughing on the gum that suddenly lodged in his throat.

Realizing Jordan had played him yet again, Brett lunged a kick at Jordan, but like the thousand times before, he missed by several feet. This time, however, rather than just hitting air as normal, he kicked the side of an empty bookshelf, causing it to topple onto one side.

Jordan dodged to avoid being crushed.

The oak bookshelf was heavy and well-constructed, so well that even after crashing to the floor, it amazingly remained in one piece.

"You idiot!" Jordan yelled. "That could've killed me!"

"So, don't mess with me like that. Now we're even."

Unable to think of a great damaging come-back quickly enough to satisfy his pride, Jordan knelt on the floor, grabbing a dilapidated book that had apparently sometime long ago fallen behind the bookshelf, and positioning the book's spine in his thumb and index finger like a knife-throwing marksmen, he hurled it at Brett, hitting his friend directly in the chest. A bull's eye.

Brett scrambled to his knees to grab the book and launch it back towards Jordan's head when he noticed a straw-like object protruding from the top of the book's spine.

Jordan stood laughing with one leg bent upwards and his arms over his face in a sarcastic display of appearing to defend himself. He knew Brett's throw would be nowhere close.

"Hey. Check this out," Brett said. Suddenly oblivious to Jordan's taunting, he walked towards the smeared window next to him and held the book up to the yellowed light.

Frayed and cracked and now in two pieces, the book's cover was embossed with the word *Algebra* in flaking gold, and protruding from its spine were small pieces of tanned paper rolled into a tube.

"So, it's a cheap old book falling apart. Big deal," Jordan said.

Brett carefully pulled the paper tube from the top of the book and unrolled it.

It was a letter.

"What's it say?" Jordan asked.

Brett read it aloud.

To my esteemed and respected colleague, literary executor, et al.,
Mr. Rufus Griswold:

It has been my honor to have you as an adversary throughout our respective literary careers. I now call on you as a friend. I am most indebted to you for honoring my request that you serve as my literary executor. I again entrust you to tell the world of me what I could not.

You have made many remarks–biting as they often were–of my fondness—dare you say—of my <u>obsession</u> with the cryptogram, the cipher. Even as the faithful man reads the Holy Book, he is inspired to deeper thinking beyond what he finds on the printed page. He uncovers that which he never saw before, yet was there all the while. I have endeavored to do the same in my work.

In many of my writings, I labored intently and methodically to bury a message of some nature longing to be exhumed. The reader educated in the fine arts of coding and encryption will find a message divorced from the tone and mood of the work. I began this diversion simply for my own amusement and to humor the trained eye, as the codes referred to some geographical location familiar to my own person, or perhaps familiar to the reader. But as my years passed, alas, as my fortunes turned to darker days, I found usefulness in this folly.

A sympathetic former publisher, or one whose guilt-ridden conscience became an unbearable companion, presented me with a small portion of the earnings from the sale of some of my lesser works owned by the said publisher. It was not a fortune, but it was enough for a rebirth, a second chance for a life of fewer demons and phantoms. So with the legion of memories that haunt me, I entombed this fruit of my life's work in a safe location near my destination. I appear as a pauper on the edge of ruin to those who know me. But is there not always more to see than what you see? Is not the artist who starves held in more sympathy and martyrdom than the one wallowing in his wealth? I have been called on occasion a charlatan. What if this title holds true? What if my austere appearance is but an illusion painted? I leave it for you to decipher.

Here is my challenge to you, if you have the bravado to commit your energies to my insanity. I have included with this document a series of clues to unlocking the hidden mysteries within the works, clues to the clues, if you will. Should you find the prize at the end of the quest, consider it payment for writing my biography after I cross over to the land of the forbidden knowledge.

May your odyssey lead to the hero's end.

I am, respectfully,

E. A. P.

"So who's E.A.P.?" Jordan asked, taking the other paper Brett held in his hand, a page imprinted with long columns of numbers.

"I don't know. Look it up on your phone."

Jordan handed the numbered paper back to Brett and began tapping his phone face.

"I'm getting *employee assistance program* and *extensible authentication protocol,* whatever that is. No names."

"Try *Rufus Griswold.*"

"How do you spell it?"

Brett pointed to the name on the letter.

"Okay. He was a writer who lived in the 1800s. It says he was a rival with—Edgar Allan Poe."

"Edgar Allan Poe," Brett repeated. "E.A.P. . .there's no way. That can't be it."

"Can't be what?"

"It can't really be him. Edgar Allan Poe."

"Who's that?"

"Seriously?"

"Yeah. I'm serious. Who is he?"

"Language arts? The guy who wrote 'The Raven'? 'The Tell-Tale Heart'? 'Black Cat'?"

"Oh, him. Yeah. I didn't get into that much."

"Anyway, if he really wrote this, can you imagine how much this thing is worth?"

"Not really. So what do we do with it?"

"Good question. We can ask my dad about it and see what he thinks. It might be worth some serious money. We'll be able to set our price."

But they had no idea the price they would pay for finding it.

XSZKGVI 2

"So, what do you think, Tom?" Brett's father asked as he placed the paper on the table.

"Hard to tell. The ink seems to date to around the late 1840s, according to the gas chromatograph."

Jordan and Brett were amazed that someone with Dr. Laurence's expertise would take the time to answer their questions. Tom Laurence was an associate professor of chemistry at Friedman University, and while the college was relatively unknown, Dr. Laurence wasn't. His expertise was in ink chemical analysis; he was one of the few experts in the region specializing in thin-layer chromatography, a profession sure to be a discussion-killer in social situations, yet a precious commodity in legal cases involving forgery, counterfeiting, and falsifying documents.

"So do you think it could be legitimate?" Dr. Kerchoff asked.

"Well, here's the deal," Dr. Laurence said after most of his sip of coffee dripped onto his tie, blending with the mosaic of impressionistic art derived from coffee stains. "I scanned the initials and sent it with another signature to a friend of mine who teaches at Purdue."

"Another signature?" Brett asked.

"Yeah, I had the Archives Department here on campus send over a scan of one of Poe's signatures on a rejection letter they've got in their collection that he sent to some poor want-to-be writer. One of their staff members said that Poe was an editor of a literary magazine for a while in charge of accepting stories and articles. I honestly don't know all that much about Poe," Dr. Laurence said. "I haven't really thought about him since junior high."

"So why two signatures?" Jordan asked.

"In an experiment, you always have to have a control, right? Well, I sent both so I could be sure she was giving me an accurate analysis, although I didn't tell her which was which. I just told her one was authentic and one was a forgery. Since the ink tested to the correct time period, I couldn't make a solid conclusion, which meant I'd need help in interpreting Poe's signature traits. I guess you could say my friend is a bit of a Poe enthusiast. Here, I'll pull up the email and you can see what she said. You sort of have to excuse her because she tends to get carried away a bit when you get her talking about Poe."

They crowded around the monitor as Dr. Laurence read the email aloud.

Tom:

This is an interesting specimen. Both signatures you sent appear to have been written sometime near the end of Poe's life. He did extensive studies of people's handwriting and actually thought he could analyze a person's character by their signature, like many did at the time, a technique which they called autography. Poe was known to change his signature often so it would be difficult for anyone to analyze his own writing.

So which of the signatures is authentic? I ran both samples through a program I'm developing and cross-referenced them with my own visual observation. My results show that Specimen A (the signature) is authentic and Specimen B (the initials) is improbable. I have attached the analysis results to this message. Let me know if you have any further questions.

Take care,

Monique Locard

Associate Professor of Forensic Chemistry

Department of Chemistry

Purdue University

West Lafayette, Indiana

"So there you go. Sorry, guys. Looks like you found an antique idea of someone's practical joke," Dr. Laurence said, rubbing his glasses with the only coffee-free spot on his tie.

"You know, when you think about it, it wouldn't really make sense that Edgar Allan Poe—who lived on the East Coast, I'm assuming—would hide papers like these in a plain algebra book anyway," Brett's dad said. "You'd think he'd be pretty anxious about getting them to this Griswold as fast as he could."

He watched as the boys' disappointment shadowed their optimistic faces, visions of their piles of money fizzling like dying bottle rockets as the sobering truth of ice-cold data callously stared them in the face.

"But, hey. What do I know, right? I'm an anthropology professor, not a literary scholar. I've seen crazier things happen that defied the logic and the data."

"You never know, guys," Dr. Laurence added. "If anything, it'd be interesting to see how the codes work out, so I've made some copies of these lists of numbers. I'd like to see what you might be able to do with it, you know, see if there is any truth in the letter anyway. Even if the writer wasn't really Edgar Allan Poe. Who knows? Monique's data might be way off, and we might be eating our words in the end."

"I've got to stick around and get some work done," Dr. Kerchoff said. "So why don't you guys get something to eat over at The Commons while you're here. Here's some money. You can pay me back when you've found the Ark of the Covenant."

Both boys looked at Brett's dad, confused.

"Indiana Jones? *Raiders of the Lost Ark*? The movie?"

"Oh, yeah," they both said. Between the two, only Jordan knew what Dr. Kerchoff was talking about.

"Thanks, Dad. And thanks, Dr. Laurence, for all the hassle you went through to check this out."

"Not a problem, Brett. I'm really curious to see where this might go."

The automatic door swished shut behind the boys as they left the lab.

XSZKGVI 3

Brett and Jordan took the elevator to the main floor, trying desperately to convince themselves that they weren't disappointed. Both were failing deplorably.

Jordan made a feeble attempt to change the subject.

"It was pretty nice of your dad to ask Dr. Laurence to have his friend run those tests," he said, blindly staring at the elevator inspection card fixed above the button panel.

Brett did not respond.

"And giving us money for lunch," Jordan added.

"Whatever."

"What do you mean?"

"So Dad gave us money. Great. He's a great guy."

"What's your problem?"

"My problem? He's the problem. I hate when he pulls that."

"Pulls what?"

"Acting all concerned and joking around and all that, like he really cares. He doesn't care. He's hardly ever home, and when he is, his face is shoved into his laptop doing work. You're never around to see the real thing."

"He seems all right when I'm over at your house," Jordan said, not sure whose side he should take.

"It's an act. Every time I ask him something, he tells me we'll see later, if he even says anything at all. I mean, he doesn't beat me or anything like that. He just ignores me, then pretends he's all Mr. Dad when other people are around. He doesn't even look at me most of the time."

Jordan didn't respond. Didn't know how to respond. Brett had never expressed such deep emotions concerning his father before, and Jordan was stunned to hear him berate Dr. Kerchoff like he just had. He'd never known. Friends nearly their entire life, and he'd never really known.

Uneasy and unsure, Jordan made the safe shift and changed the subject as the boys stepped out of the elevator and walked across the campus quad, an open area where a mosaic of light and dark gray brick pavement with large cubical stones were stacked arbitrarily here and there, making the plaza resemble a natural stone quarry. A waterfall rolled down the side of one of the more orderly stacks; on the opposite side, a concrete slab canopied an area containing metal benches and tables.

"Well, I still don't care," he said. "I think Dr. Laurence's friend at Purdue is wrong."

Grateful for Jordan's detour in the uncomfortable conversation, Brett responded. "You're right. I mean, she really didn't give any details about the results. And Dr. Laurence said the ink was old enough to be real. But who cares? I say we mess with it and see what happens."

"Can you imagine if it actually was for real? That there was some kind of reward or treasure or something? We could be rich!" Jordan said, nearly shoving Brett into a metal bench as they walked. "What would you do with your cut of the money?"

"We'd better get it first, if there actually is anything. But what if we go through all this and waste a whole summer and Dr. Laurence's friend *is* right?"

"Who cares? It'll be worth a try. Sometimes you just got to take a chance," Jordan said, smiling at two college girls sitting at one of the outdoor tables.

"Hey, my name's Jordan Hebern, and I'm probably going to be pretty rich soon. I'll look you two up in a couple of years, okay?"

"Shut up!" Brett hissed.

"Why? They were hot. Who cares?"

"We're junior high kids. We're like little babies to them."

"Well, they can put me on their lap anytime they want."

The boys' laughter echoed underneath the concrete overhang of the Student Commons.

XSZKGVI 4

"Here are the copies Dad made for us," Brett said, sliding the papers across the lunch room table to Jordan.

"So what are we looking for?"

"Well, the letter said these are clues to clues. So I'm guessing what we need to do is solve the first clue to get to the next one."

"Where are they?" Jordan asked. "All I see is a bunch of numbers."

"I know. This makes no sense. This stuff's impossible."

Brett stared at the page partially covered by his hamburger and fries. As the lunch crowd of students taking summer classes began to trickle into the restaurant and walk past their table, Brett felt the urge to hide the page, as if compelled to conceal some form of forbidden knowledge or some sensitive confidential document.

Ironically, he had no idea what he was trying to hide or why he was trying to hide it.

At the top of the page were the words "*En regle est la seule maniere*," followed by a series of numbers: 26 25 26 13 23 12 13 19 12 11 22 26 15 15 2 22 4 19 12 22 13 7 22 9 19 22 9 22 12 13 15 2 7 19 22 21 15 26 14 22 4 18 15 15 25 22 2 12 6 9 20 26 7 22. The rest of the page was blank.

And for several minutes, so were both boys' brains.

"Wait a minute," Jordan said suddenly, staring intently at the paper. "Give me a pen."

"What for?"

"Just give me the pen. I think I found something."

On the blank area of the copy, Jordan began writing the alphabet. Then starting with *z*, he wrote a number under each letter,

1 under z, 2 under y, ending with *26 under a.*

Brett stared at his friend's frantic scribbling, stunned to see Jordan so engrossed, so focused, so determined, so sure.

He substituted the letters written under each number for the numbers themselves and rewrote his work, trying to break the letters into words.

"There you go," Jordan said, shoving the paper across the table to Brett as casually as if he had just written his locker combination.

It read *Abandon hope, all ye who enter here. Only the flame will be your gate.*

"How'd you do that?" Brett asked.

"*Wheel of Fortune.*"

"What?"

"*Wheel of Fortune.* Don't you ever watch it?"

"Not really. I think it's pretty stupid."

"You would. Anyway, back in the old days of the show, like the eighties and nineties, on the final bonus round, you had to pick five letters and a vowel to solve the puzzle. They give them to you now, but back then everybody that wasn't an idiot would always pick *r, s, t, l, n,* and *e.*"

"Why?" Brett asked, increasingly amazed at Jordan's sudden surge of intellect.

Jordan smirked. "Because, honors student genius, those letters are the most used letters in the alphabet. See how those numbers repeat here? I figured they had to be those letters, or at least some of them. See how the number *22* is used more than the others? I figured it had to be *e.* So I counted through the alphabet to *e,* which would make it *5.* But *5* isn't even used at all. So then I went backwards, which makes *e* the number *22.* After that, I looked for *26,* which would be *a.* Then everything started falling into place."

"Are you kidding me? You figured all of that out that fast? Seriously?"

"You got school brains. I got real-life brains."

"So what does it mean?"

"Don't ask me. I just figured it out. It's your turn now."

"But that's all there is to it. We're going to have to get some help. There's no way we can figure this out on our own."

"We've got all summer. Want to go over to the RFC and shoot around? They just got the new rims up."

Both were putting their trash on their trays when Brett suddenly froze.

"What's your problem?" Jordan asked.

"Lauren's here."

"Great. Here we go. Why don't you just ask her?"

"I can't."

"You want me to do it for you? I mean, it's not that hard."

"No! Here she comes. Jordan, I mean it. Don't say anything."

"Fine. But I'm telling you, you are such an idiot."

Lauren could have easily been mistaken for one of the college students on campus as she walked across the commons towards the restaurant, her only giveaway being a constant glance around her, as if she were acutely aware of her surroundings, unlike the regular summer students who either gazed straight ahead to avoid eye contact with others, or focused on their phones in their hands. She wore little make up. As far as Brett was concerned, she didn't have to wear any.

"Hey, guys, what are you doing here?" Lauren asked, tucking a strand of her red hair behind her ear.

Brett avoided looking her directly in the eyes. They were so blue, he always caught himself staring into them, always amazed that eyes could be that color with that many tiny sparkles in them, and he didn't want to give her the impression he was some sort of creep. He had liked Lauren Karga since the second grade, when their desks were arranged in pairs, and since their names were together alphabetically (Karga and Kerchoff), Brett knew they were destined to be together, as they were in any school situation requiring student sorting. A line. A roster. An order. Always together. K and K. A relationship built on a foundation even more solid than the multiplication table.

The alphabet.

Lauren was different from almost every other girl at Mitchell Kinnaird Junior High, at least from those who tried to pretend they were someone they weren't. The attractive girls knew they were attractive and assumed everyone else knew it as well. Most of them savored every flirt directed at them, every stare, every accidental bump in the hall. But they acted like they detested it, like it nauseated them that someone of a lower class would even dare to invade their personal space. They were in a different league, and they knew it.

Lauren was the exception. She knew she was pretty — girls with her beauty are well aware of their looks—but Lauren never made an issue of it. In truth, she was embarrassed by her own attractiveness. She often cringed when someone complimented her, though not in an arrogant manner, as if she thought the person paying the compliment was beneath her, like many of the other girls who secretly resented Lauren for her appearance. Some even hated her, interpreting her humility as artificial, a thin mask to hide her conceit. That beauty was more of a curse for Lauren than it was an asset made her all the more attractive to Brett.

"Uh, my dad had to do some work in his office, so he let Jordan and me come over to shoot around at the Fitness Center," Brett said, desperately and awkwardly avoiding direct eye contact with Lauren.

"How come you're here?" Jordan asked, realizing Brett had no intention of continuing the conversation. He knew he would have to cover Brett's back, save him again from another self-inflicted catastrophe. *What a wimp*, he thought.

"We're going to the pool after my sister's class, so we're just sort of hanging out until it's over."

Then there was silence, the suffocating, nerve-wrenching dead space in a conversation when nothing is exchanged, when both sides desperately hope the other fills the void so they won't have to. After several seconds of Lauren and Brett avoiding direct looks or any kind of verbal exchange, it was more than Jordan could stand.

"So, do you know anything about Edgar Allan Poe?" Jordan asked Lauren, his sudden burst of communication startling her and infuriating Brett.

Brett envisioned himself smashing his tray full-force into Jordan's face. But as was typical with his luck, he would successfully knock Jordan out, only for Lauren to come to Jordan's aid, prompting them to fall in love, date in high school, go the prom together, go to the same college, get married, and have about twenty-seven children (all with red hair), and every evening they would all watch *Wheel of Fortune* together and live happily ever after. Brett was in no way going to allow Jordan to steal her, so he let his flash-forward of the future fade away, resolving only to give his pal a cold death-stare.

"Poe? Seriously? He's only like one of my favorite authors. I've read almost all of his stuff. It's pretty weird and creepy, and his style is old, but you get used to it. Did you know that they don't even know if it's really him buried under his tombstone? There's this theory that when they wanted to relocate his body to a new grave, they messed up and . . ."

Brett didn't hear a word, only her voice. She was unbelievable. He wished he had it in him to tell her how he really felt, how he had always felt, but he knew in reality he didn't have a chance with her. Girls like Lauren didn't have it for guys like him.

But maybe one day.

Maybe.

Suddenly Lauren started to feel silly rattling on. "I'm sorry. I'm sort of a freak, I know. But I think stuff like that is so cool. So what were you wanting to know about Poe?"

At that point, Jordan knew Brett was ready to thrash him in an enraged frenzy.

"Well, we found this—this trivia contest online. It's for some gift certificates or something," Jordan lied, and did a horrible job of it.

"Hey, whatever I can do to help, just let me know."

Lauren waited for a response, an invitation to sit down, to go to the gym with them, to talk more about Poe, anything—whatever it took—to get to spend at least a few more minutes with them. With Brett. Her mother had taught her that girls should never make the first move, but Brett had yet to make even one. She had attempted every angle she knew to get his attention, every trick to get him to talk to her, but he avoided her every time. He wasn't interested, she was well aware of it, and sometime, somehow, someway, she'd get over it. Get over him.

Easier said than done.

Just as Lauren was starting to feel the awkwardness of the moment, she found a quick out. "I think I see my sister. I'll see you guys around. Let me know if you need any help on the contest."

"See you," Jordan said.

Lauren exited through the glass door and walked across the Commons. She glanced over her shoulder just before she turned the corner out of sight.

"You're an idiot," Jordan said. "That's all there is to it. An absolute idiot. What's wrong with you?"

"What?"

"You know what. She wanted you to talk to her."

"Whatever."

"You know, for someone as smart as you are, you are so stupid. She likes you. She was waiting for you to say something to her."

"Sure."

"Fine. I'm done. But when she gets a boyfriend and you're sitting there picking your nose wondering what happened, I don't want to hear it. So, go ahead. Be an idiot."

"At least I wasn't stupid enough to almost tell her about the letter."

"What? Come on. That was the perfect door. But if you're not going to ask her out, then we should at least get her to help us. She sounds like she knows what she's talking about."

"Do you really think she likes me?" Brett couldn't convince himself it might be even remotely true.

"If you're too dumb to see it, then I can't help you. Ask your dad if you can come over tonight, and we'll ask Lauren too so she can help."

"I don't have her number," said Brett.

"No problem. I've got it."

"Seriously? How did *you* get it?"

"We were working on a lab in science a few months ago."

"And she actually gave you her number. So you could text her?"

"Yeah. So what? You want it?"

"No," Brett replied.

"Man, you really are an idiot," Jordan said.

XSZKGVI 5

Brett: Wats up?

Lauren: nm...Hbu?

Brett: J and me r @ my hous

Lauren: K

Brett: were u 4 real bout helpin us w/ the Poe thing?

Lauren: I'd <3 to! :)

Brett: kk..u know how we told u that we were in tht contest? thts not true. we found a note and were kinda sure it was by Poe.

Lauren: Wat!?

Brett: we think its real

Lauren: wats it say?????

Brett: it leads to a treasure!!

Lauren: re u kidding?! really?? awesome!!! Do you think I could see it? :)

Brett: yeah!!

Lauren: when???

Brett: well wat are u doin tmrw?

Lauren: nothing now . . .

Brett: can we meet up @ Central Library?

Lauren: time ....??

Brett: how about 10ish?

Lauren: kk. wat do I need??

Brett: ur brain duh! haha lol

Lauren: lol!! G2G!! see u tmrw! :)

Brett: Cya!!

XSZKGVI 6

"Here's what we've got so far," Brett said, laying two sheets of paper on the library computer-lab table, a copy of the forged Poe letter and the decoded message. Brett tried to whisper, not as much out of respect for the other library visitors, but to keep his voice from echoing off the granite floor and plaster walls. The building still looked much like its pictures from the 1920s, marble drinking fountains, wooden trimmed check-out counter; even the elevator to the third floor still had the grated door that had to be hand-closed.

"This letter explains everything, but we can't figure out this sentence."

Lauren read the letter's contents. "It's true," she said.

"What is?"

"Rufus Griswold. Poe really asked him. He was a writer who was an off-and-on friend and enemy of Poe's," Lauren replied, not looking up from the letter in her hand. "He wrote Poe's biography a few years after he died, but Griswold really hated him then, so he made up a bunch of lies to make Poe look bad."

"How come?" Jordan asked.

"To get even with him. Poe said some pretty bad things about Griswold's writing, so this was Griswold's way of getting even. They think he even took some of Poe's letters and rewrote them so it'd make his friends hate him, too. In fact, a lot of the rumors about Poe, like he was a drug addict, and that he was insane, were in the book Griswold wrote about him, and most of the stuff's not even true."

"Did Poe feel the same way about Griswold?" Brett asked.

"Sort of. But not as much. But it looks like from this letter that he liked Griswold enough to let him decide how history would remember him."

"Do you think it's the real thing, then?" Jordan asked.

"Well, the writing sounds like how Poe wrote, so I'd say it probably is."

"You know we had some tests run on it, and it shows up as being a fake, right?" Brett asked.

"Yeah, but you never know. Tests always have the chance of being wrong."

If Brett had any guts in him whatsoever, he would have kissed her right then and there. On the lips.

Jordan jumped in. "Okay, then, what if this Griswold was the one who wrote the letter, you know, like to himself, so it would look like Poe wanted him to have the money, or whatever it is, all along? What if it's all a setup?"

Jordan suspected just about every concept or object out of the ordinary had some kind of a conspiracy buried somewhere within it.

"But that wouldn't make any sense," Brett replied. "Because why would Griswold go through all that trouble just to make up a bunch of codes? He could have just written the letter so it read like Poe gave the money straight up to him."

"Oh, yeah. I didn't think about that," Jordan said. "Never mind."

"So let's figure on the letter being real," Lauren added, "which means if it is, we've got to figure out what the second paper is all about."

"Okay, so what's *that* mean? We couldn't figure it out." Jordan pointed to the heading at the top of the second page, the inscription *En regle est la seule maniere.*

"Let's find out."

Lauren took her phone out of her pocket, opened her translation app and typed in the words *En regle est la seule maniere.*

"What's it say?" Brett asked, looking over Lauren's shoulder. Her hair smelled like fruit. He wasn't sure what kind, but it didn't matter. She could actually be wearing fruit on her head, and she'd still be gorgeous.

The results confused all three of them.

"I don't get it," Brett said.

"Me neither," said Lauren.

The words *In order is the only way: translated from French* glowed from the phone screen.

"What order?" Jordan asked. "There isn't any order because there isn't anything else on the page except for that other part."

"Yeah, what does that mean?" Brett asked Lauren. "You got any ideas?"

"No, but I can find out. How'd you guys figure out that code?"

"Jordan did it. Tell her, Jordan."

"Okay, so I saw that some of the numbers were used more than others, and I figured that the most used number probably was the letter *e*, you know, like how on *Wheel of Fortune* the most common vowel is *e*."

"Like 'The Gold Bug'! Oh, wow!"

"What?" Brett and Jordan asked together.

"'The Gold Bug.' It's one of Poe's stories about this guy named William Legrand, who's looking for a buried treasure. He gets this secret code written on a piece of parchment and has to break it to find the treasure. The code, I mean. He figures it out almost just like how you did with the letter *e*. This is getting seriously interesting."

She typed the words *Abandon hope all ye who enter here* into

Google. About nine million hits matched the search, nearly all of them referring in some way to *The Divine Comedy,* by Dante. She clicked on the first entry.

"Weird," Lauren said. "It says these words are carved over the entrance to Hell in Dante's story. It's about a guy who visits Hell and sees what things are like there. It's a pretty old story."

"Okay, so what if Poe's just putting that in there just to mess with Griswold, like daring him or something?" Jordan asked.

"He might," Brett said, "but the next part is what really doesn't make any sense. *'Only the flame will be your gate.'*"

"What's he talking about?" Brett asked Lauren. "That's all there is on the rest of the page."

"There's got to be more to it. We've got to be missing something," Brett said.

"Hey, wait a minute," Jordan said. "I saw this movie once where these guys were trying to read this secret message they got by holding it up to a candle. It was written in lemon juice or something, you know, like some sort of invisible ink. Maybe the rest of the message is something like that."

"Oh my gosh! Jordan!" Lauren exclaimed. "You're a genius! It makes sense! 'Abandon hope all ye who enter here. Only the flame will be your gate.' It's just like 'The Gold Bug' again! In that story, they only find the message when they hold the paper up next to the fire. The heat makes the ink appear. That's what lemon juice does. He's saying that it's hopeless if we just read the paper like it is. We need heat for our gate—for our entrance to the rest. Brett, you've still got the original paper don't you?"

"Yeah. They put it in storage for us in the archives at the University."

"We need to see that paper again. Up close and for real."

XSZKGVI 7

"You're wanting to take a look at it again?" Dr. Laurence said as he opened the narrow drawer and extracted a flat Lexan box while Lauren, Jordan, and Brett encircled the lab table. "It's a pretty cool artifact, even if it's not authentic."

The Archives Department at the University was actually the official holding facility of all important State documents, like the original handwritten Indiana Constitution of 1816, old letters from government officials, even a few love letters from Abraham Lincoln to his wife Mary Todd. Delegated by the State to serve as the custodian of such substantial relics, Friedman University was also granted generous funding in order to execute such an immense responsibility, obtaining the means to build an advanced facility containing the most up-to-date climate control and document preservation technology available.

"So how are things going with the decryption?" Dr. Laurence asked, slipping on a pair of thin white cotton gloves.

"We need to check something out," Brett said. "Amazingly, Jordan was the one who got us finally going somewhere with it, and Lauren helped too."

"Yeah. And you said I was wasting my time watching all those movies and TV. Looks like it's paying off," Jordan replied.

Although acutely disinterested in nearly anything school-related and barely maintaining passing grades, Jordan was an honors student in movies and television. He knew at least something about nearly every film and television show ever made, especially in the genre of the lower-budget, lesser-known movies that more than likely went straight to DVD, the producers realistic enough to avoid the embarrassment of an actual theater release. Action and mysteries were his specialties.

Dr. Laurence pressed the small button that released the vacuum in the flat box, carefully lifted the papers from their container, and placed them on the exam table.

"You wouldn't happen to have any candles around here, would you, Dr. Laurence?" Brett asked. "Or maybe something that makes a flame?"

"In here? Around thousands of priceless paper documents?" He laughed. "Actually, I love my job and hope to keep it for a while . . . wait a minute . . . I know what you're thinking."

"It's the only thing that makes any sense." Brett replied. "The rest of that page has to be in—"

"Invisible ink," Dr. Laurence finished the sentence, his eyes widening. "Are you sure you want to try to do something like that? You know it will probably ruin the parchment, right?"

"We don't know what else to do," Lauren said.

"What made you think that part of this might be written in invisible ink?" Dr. Laurence asked.

"Have you ever read 'The Gold Bug'?"

"Maybe in junior high, and if I did, I don't remember much about it. Actually, I don't remember anything about it other than the title."

"It's one of Poe's stories. There's a character in it who finds a treasure map, and the only way to read it is to hold it up to heat."

"We obviously don't keep candles around here, but we do have a specimen oven. Tell you what. I'll run it through a cycle and see what happens. But I can't promise you anything. Just give me a few minutes, okay?"

Dr. Laurence carefully returned the documents to the box, placed it on the stainless steel specimen cart, and wheeled it out of the lab.

"What do we do if nothing shows up? Jordan asked.

"I guess we can't do anything, other than know that this was just another one of those things about Poe that adds to the mysterious stories and legends," Lauren said. "Even if it's not true. But it's still fun trying."

"Why are people so into Poe anyway? I mean, he's just another dead author we have to study in school," Brett said.

"A lot of people say Poe really wasn't all that great of a writer, but it was just that he was so intelligent. The stuff he wrote about was like, never done before, you know? I mean, no one really even knows how he died," Lauren replied.

"What are you talking about?" Jordan asked.

"Well, like how they found him right before he died," Lauren said. "He was missing for a couple of days and then shows up outside of a tavern in Baltimore, Maryland, lying in the gutter. They said he was like, almost unconscious and all dirty and wearing someone else's clothes which didn't even fit him. No one still really has any idea what happened to him. Some people say that elections were going on in Baltimore that day and that maybe the politicians hired some guys to get people like Poe drunk and use them to go around to different voting places and vote for the same guy. They would have them change clothes at each voting place so no one would get suspicious."

"I never heard that before," Brett said.

"There's some pretty weird stories around Poe. There's one which even says he faked his death, and it was actually someone who looked like him they buried."

"Weren't you telling us about that the other day? I don't remember what you said." Brett was genuinely interested, and he could never hear too much of Lauren's voice.

"Oh. About the tombstone? Yeah. When Poe died, he didn't have any money for a normal burial, so at first, his grave was unmarked. A few years later, some fans of his got some money together and wanted to build a monument in honor of him, which meant they'd have to move his body. When the guys got the cemetery map, they didn't know that all the graves had the feet facing the tombstone, not the head like normal, which meant they might have dug up the wrong person. You know, like digging up the guy *behind* Poe's grave. So, they don't even know if it really is Poe who's buried in his own grave. That might have started the story about him faking his death. I'm not for sure."

"How can you be so interested in all that stuff?" Jordan asked. "Doesn't it sort of creep you out?"

"Not really. I love it. I like all the mystery around it."

Dr. Laurence returned with the parchments on a metal tray. "Well, I kept it in for as long as I could without damaging it, but I think you guys might have hit a dead end," he tossed his keys onto his desk and walked to the exam table. "Nothing happened. But let me show you something." He placed the yellowed parchment under the large magnifying lens attached to the table top. "See this area under the heading? Well, this is where the charring should have happened if it was written in lemon juice or vinegar, either one."

"Charring?" Jordan asked. "You mean like burned?"

"Sort of. But not burned. Charred. What happens with this so-called invisible ink is that most of the time you need a heat source to make the ink appear. Lemon juice or vinegar are what they mainly use for invisible ink. When they heat up, it chars over before the paper does. That's why I had to stop before it caught on fire. I hate to be the one to have to break it to you, guys, but nothing showed up."

"There's got to be more," Lauren said, turning the paper over in her gloved hands. "The heading said 'Only the flame will be your gate.' It has to be heat. An actual flame will burn it up. There's got to be more. But the whole page is blank. There's nothing on it."

She laid the parchment back on the exam table and put her hands to her face in frustration and apparent defeat. Maybe Dr. Kerchoff and Dr. Laurence were right. No. They *were* right. It really was nothing after all. Somebody had scored a very convincing hoax, and she and her friends had fallen for it. But, fortunately, they had debunked it early on, before they wasted an entire summer chasing phantoms. Still, it had been worth the effort.

At least she had gotten to spend a few days with Brett.

Lauren was unable to stop thinking about him lately, and she was equally unable to discern why. He was far from athletic, but he was smart, although not a genius. It might have been the way he acted around her. She was used to guys doing stupid things to get her attention, making rude comments to her with the mistaken idea they were impressing her. But Brett would hardly look at her most of the time, and when he did, he rarely — if ever — made eye contact with her.

Perhaps this was what her aunt meant when she was talking to Lauren about how to respond to boys. The ones flirting all the time, acting like idiots, are mostly losers just hoping to get lucky. For the most part, they figure the only way they can get a girl is to impress her, to trick her into thinking they're really someone special. The ones who avoid girls, who shy away from them, seem embarrassed around them, her aunt said, are the ones you've got to pay attention to, get to know a little. A lot of the times, those are the ones that will treat you right.

All Brett had to do was ask.

Jordan leaned over the table for a closer look at the parchment paper, not really knowing why, other than perhaps out of hope. His leg inadvertently bumped the switch controlling the recessed light beneath the Plexiglas table top that functioned much like an old overhead projector.

"Oops. Sorry about that," Jordan said, quickly pressing the switch a second time, turning off the light.

"Wait! Do that again!" Brett shouted. "Turn it back on!"

"Why?"

"Just do it!" Brett yelled again.

Jordan felt for the switch under the table and quickly pressed it again, resisting the urge to begin flipping it on and off like a huge strobe light.

A one hundred thousand dollar strobe light.

No one said a word when the enlarged image of the document was projected on the entire front wall of the lab.

"Okay, so maybe I was wrong," Dr. Laurence said quietly. "Wow."

Nearly filling the entire empty space on the page were several columns of symbols, similar to a word search puzzle, with the exceptions that the first three columns were letters, the rest numbers, and that every other symbol was inverted — backwards.

"Jordan, you need to screw up more often," Brett said.

"Let me see the parchment again for a second." Dr. Laurence took the document off the exam table and placed it under an enlarger, a bizarre-looking device comparable to a microscope. "How could I have missed this?" he said, peering into the eyepiece.

"Missed what?" Lauren asked.

"Check this out."

Dr. Laurence switched the viewer to a monitor next to the scope. "There are two parchments here."

"Two papers?" Brett replied.

"Parchments. That's why it works so well. Look. See the edge of where that little rip is? When I zoom in, you can see there are two layers of parchment. I don't know how in the world they sealed it as well as they did. I can't believe the Archives Department didn't catch it."

"So how does it work?" Jordan asked.

"It looks like whoever did this took two sheets of parchment and wrote the codes on the one side and spaced the letters and numbers evenly so that they'd line up in the spaces of the letters and numbers on the other parchment," Dr. Laurence said. "Then somehow, they adhered the two face to face so the backs of each sheet faced out. Hold it in your hands, and it looks like just a blank sheet of paper. Which makes sense why every other symbol is backwards."

"Now I get it. 'Only the flame will be your guide.' It wasn't the *heat* of a flame—it was its *light*. You've got to hold it up to light to read it. I get it," Brett said.

"So we've got the whole thing, now, but how are we supposed to figure out what the rest of it says?" Jordan asked.

"Good question," Brett replied.

The four focused on the three columns of letters, hoping that they would somehow reveal a hint as to their meaning, which at the moment looked like nothing more than an ordered mess of nothing.

"Guys, I've got a lab to supervise in fifteen minutes, so I've got to head out," Dr. Laurence said. "I know Monique's test results show the letter is fake, but I still think this is pretty amazing. Intriguing, if anything. Good luck. Be sure to put the document back in the case when you're finished. I'll put it back and shut everything down when my lab is over."

"No problem," Brett replied.

"See you, Dr. Laurence. Thanks for all the help," Jordan said.

"Anytime. Just remember to include me in the credits when they make the movie about this, okay? See you."

XSZKGVI 8

The three stared, scribbled, and scratched for what seemed like an eternity, desperate to make any kind of sense—however miniscule—of the symbols glaring back at them, taunting them.

"Wait. I think I've got it," Brett said suddenly. He turned to the board behind him and began writing on it with the dry erase marker he found on the desk. "If you start at the bottom and go back and forth across the columns, I think it might work. I think the first word is *the*. Lauren, write down these letters when I say them, would you? Your handwriting is better than Jordan's. See if you can separate them into words."

"Okay."

"So what about all those numbers?" Jordan asked.

"We'll worry about those when we get to them." Brett began calling off the letters as he followed the pattern in the columns. When he had exhausted all the columns, he asked Lauren, "What did you come up with?"

"Well," she answered, "It looks like it breaks down into *the ominous bird of yore shall be your Charon across the Plutonian shore. The letter the word the syllable fit as an equation.*"

"Great. Does this guy ever write anything that makes sense?" Jordan said.

"Do you have a copy of the poem?" Brett asked Lauren, knowing she was thinking exactly the same thing.

"Yep." She opened the app on her phone screen. "Right here. In *The Complete Works of Edgar Allan Poe.*"

"What are you two talking about?" Jordan exclaimed, perturbed that he suddenly found himself outside of the circle, the very circle he had been trying to create around Lauren and Brett all this time, yet never envisioning himself apart from it, the creator separated from his creation. "You mean you two figured it out already?"

"It's easy, Jordan," Lauren said. "The 'ominous bird of yore' is how the narrator in 'The Raven' describes the bird that flies into his living room through his window."

"You mean that poem we had to read in language arts? About 'nevermore' and all that?"

"That's the one."

"I hated reading it. Mrs. Savelle said the poem was supposed to give people nightmares when they read it back then, but there wasn't anything scary about some bird coming in your house. The thing didn't make any sense. The rhymes weren't bad, but that was it. So what's so great about 'The Raven' that would make Poe use it for the code?"

"Seriously? It's only the most popular thing he ever wrote," Brett said, glancing at Lauren to see her reaction to his insight, at his sudden expertise in *Poeology*.

"It's still popular," Lauren added.

"Whatever."

"It is. The Baltimore Ravens football team?" Brett asked.

"Yeah. So?"

"Well, they named the team after the poem."

"You're an idiot."

"Look it up on their website sometime, then, if you don't believe me. The mascot's name is Poe. Seriously. Why would I make up something like that?"

Jordan didn't respond. But he had to admit, if it *was* true, it was pretty interesting.

"Okay, we know he's talking about 'The Raven,' right?" asked Lauren. "So he's saying the Raven, the 'bird of yore' will be our Charon. So who's Charon, or what, and what's the Plutonian shore? I mean, Poe mentions it twice in the poem, so it has to be important."

Brett went to the computer in the front of the lab and searched *definition: Charon.*

"Look. It says Charon was the guy who ran the ferry boat across the Styx River."

"I have no idea what you're talking about," Jordan said.

"It says the Greeks and Romans believed that when someone died, they had to go to the Underworld. They had to cross the underground river Styx to get there. What they would do is bury people with a coin in their mouth so they could pay Charon to take them across."

"So what does a—"

"There's more. When the three main gods were deciding what part of the world they were going to rule, Jupiter picked the sky, and Neptune picked the ocean. Since there was only one place left, Pluto was stuck with the Underworld. So I guess when Poe talks about the *Night's Plutonian shore*, he's talking about what we call Hell, or maybe some type of extreme pain or torture."

"This is really getting interesting. And a little weird," Jordan said.

"Here's what I think," Brett said. "I think what Poe's saying is that the poem itself is somehow going to guide us through the clues."

"Okay, but what about the other part?" Lauren asked. "About the letters and syllables and equation and all that?"

"Well, so far we've been pretty lucky. It can't be too hard to figure out." Brett's phone vibrated on the table next to him. He looked at the screen. "My dad says it's time to go. Lauren, you've got a ride, don't you?" he asked.

"Yeah, my sister's in the library. Do me a favor and take a picture of this code sheet and send it to me, okay?" Lauren said. "I've got a feeling I'm not going to get much sleep until I figure this thing out. I guess I'll see you guys at school Monday."

"See you," Brett replied.

He couldn't wait until Monday.

XSZKGVI 9

Brett felt like he was floating in warm yogurt.

A sudden jolt shot though every muscle in his body, causing them all to contract at once. He was afraid someone noticed, so he tried to re-enter Mrs. Savelle's captivating discussion of the fabulous semi-colon. Independent clauses, dependent clauses, Santa Clauses—everything melted back into a blur as he began to gradually lose consciousness. Again. His eyes burned. His chin felt numb where his hand held his head up, keeping it from smashing onto the desktop. His breathing deepened. He was sliding into a deep sleep, and there was no way he could stop it, no matter how hard he resisted.

They had broken the first code on Saturday. Today was Wednesday, and Brett had slept a little more than twelve hours total since. He had become obsessed with the Poe Codec, the codename they decided to call the project, or the hunt, or the enormous waste of time, whatever this was they were undertaking.

The name was Lauren's idea. She said that a *codec* is something in a computer that scrambles information before it sends it, then unscrambles it on the other end, when it is received. By definition, the codec *encoded* (co-) and *decoded* (-dec) a message, the function the poem "The Raven" served for them. Jordan argued for calling it "The Raven Codec," but Lauren suggested that having the poem's title in the name might make too much of an obvious connection.

She was a genius.

Brett could not resist relentlessly analyzing the second part of the code, and it was killing him. Almost literally, from lack of sleep.

The numbers. They tried every combination of substitution codes they knew, but even trying to find a repetitive pattern of the letter *e* like Jordan did that day in the Student Commons was leading to dead ends. Nothing made sense.

The bell tones ending the class period jolted him back to consciousness.

"And don't forget that your independent research paper is due tomorrow," Mrs. Savelle said to the backs of the twenty-six eighth graders rushing for the hallways to extract as much freedom as possible from the five minutes before the next class. She had the appearance of someone who might have been attractive in her younger years; when she smiled, her green eyes seemed to flash and the small mole on the side of her upper lip slid with her sideways grin. One of the older teachers in the building, she still dressed in younger styles, or at least tried to. Although shorter than most of her students, she could still command a presence, defaulting to humor in most cases to defuse potentially escalating situations, yet being clearly direct when necessary. The students knew Mrs. Savelle cared about them, and about their future, which was why she had only minor discipline problems in her classes.

The paper! It was due tomorrow! Brett had completely forgotten about it. He had intended to work on it over the weekend, but his attention was obviously diverted elsewhere.

"Brett, could I see you for a minute?" she asked him. He was still immersed in the groggy disorientation of just awakening and not knowing for sure where he was. A wave of panic consumed him, like all the other times a teacher asked to speak with him. Even when he had no reason for concern — typically every time — he still felt the fear.

He slowly walked to Mrs. Savelle's desk and stared at her shoulder and then the wall behind her, anywhere but her eyes.

"Brett, is there anything you'd like to talk about?"

He detested this game, when adults held a preconceived assumption of what you were going to say, and what you *should* say, yet still wanted you to confess it, wanted it to come from your own mouth. The power play. Brett decided that to end the game quickly, he might as well take the initiative to start it.

"I'm sorry for falling asleep. I've been pretty tired lately."

"Well, I know that punctuation is not something that floats most people's boats, but you've really been out of it lately."

Brett thought it was hilarious when adults attempted to make their dialogue sound young, although he didn't dare laugh. Or smile.

"I just haven't been getting much sleep the last few days, that's all."

"Look, the only reason I'm talking to you about this is because you haven't turned anything in all week. That's not you. With the missing assignments, your language arts grade has really dropped. Drastically. Is there something going on here at school that I can help you with? Any problems that might be distracting you?"

"No. Everything's okay. I've just been sort of sidetracked lately. It's kind of hard to explain."

"Okay. I respect your privacy. I don't want to pry. Just remember that if you need any help, I'm here, and if I can't help you, I can find someone who can, okay? Fair enough?"

"Yeah, thanks," Brett replied, as he walked back to his desk to get his books and tablet. He was glad the short conference was finally over.

But before he could leave, Mrs. Savelle walked to the door and pulled it shut. Brett felt his stomach drop.

"Brett, really, I don't mean to be sticking my nose into business where it doesn't belong, but what is the Poe Codec?"

Brett suddenly became nauseated.

"The what?"

"I found the note you dropped—or someone else did—outside my door yesterday. I noticed it was written in some sort of code, so I figured someone going to all that trouble was either having a lot of fun, or really trying to hide something. I couldn't help myself. I hope you'll forgive me."

"But how—"

"It's called a substitution code. It's the simplest kind of encryption there is. It means that you just substitute a symbol, or a number, or another letter for the real one. You—or whoever did—numbered letters in the alphabet, like *a* equals *1*, *b* equals *2*, and so on. I think codes are really interesting, so I translated the note just to see what it said."

Mrs. Savelle slid the wrinkled scrap of paper containing the code across her desk: 23, 8, 5, 18, 5, 1, 18, 5, 25, 15, 6, 15, 14, 20, 8, 5, 16, 15, 5, 3, 15, 4, 5, 3.

"How'd you know it was mine?"

"Because your name was in it. I've only got one Brett in all of my classes. So it is yours, right?"

The trap. He was never good at lying or even hiding the truth. Ever. Except for how he really felt about Lauren.

"Yeah, it's mine."

"It sounds interesting. I'm sorry. I shouldn't be so nosy. All the note said was 'Where are you on the Poe Codec?' I figured it was a puzzle or something, or a book a few of you were reading. I won't press you for any more of an explanation. Anyway, try and get some sleep, okay? You can still turn in those missing assignments." She handed him a scrap of paper she had signed. "Here's a pass to your next class. I'm sorry for keeping you. See you tomorrow."

She walked to the door and allowed twenty-seven more eighth graders to drag themselves in for another daily beating of language arts.

Mrs. Savelle knew about the Poe Codec.

But fortunately, not enough.

XSZKGVI 10

"Mrs. Savelle knows what we're doing," Brett said to Lauren and Jordan as the three sat at a table in the school library, intending to study for a coming social studies test. Their books lay open, unread, unstudied.

"What do you mean she knows?" Jordan asked. "How'd she find out?"

"Did you write me a note in code?"

"No. I'm not that stupid," Jordan replied.

"I am," Lauren said. "I meant to give it to you at lunch, but I lost it. I guess I know where it is now."

"Great. We don't need the whole world knowing about everything." Jordan leaned back in his chair. "The more people who get involved, the more we're going to have to divide up the money, or whatever we end up finding."

"I've been thinking about that," Brett said. "Maybe we ought to think about having Mrs. Savelle help us. I mean, she knows more about Edgar Allan Poe than all of us put together, and she knows a lot about other stuff, too. Why not let her in on it?"

"Let's see," Jordan said. "Two reasons. One, she's an adult. And two, she's a teacher. Need any more?"

"Brett is right, Jordan. She could definitely help us out, and I don't think she'd go around telling everybody, either. Not that what we're doing is anything major. I think we should let her."

"I don't," Jordan answered.

"Come on, Jordan, think about it," Brett said. "We're stuck.

We've spent almost a week on this second part, and we've gotten nowhere. We're going to have to get some help somewhere."

"Ask your dad," Jordan said. "He'd know."

"Forget my dad. He's got some project he's working on at the University right now, so he's gone most of the time. And even if he was around, he wouldn't help us anyway." Brett spat the words as he spoke, as if they were bitter seeds, which they were to him.

"Why are you so hard on your dad?" Jordan asked. "He's actually pretty cool."

"Anyway," Brett said, attempting to divert the conversation to avoid an embarrassing tirade in front of Lauren. "Mrs. Savelle teaches Poe every year. She's got to know a lot about him."

"Please, Jordan," said Lauren. "We can just ask her about stuff we can't figure out. She's okay. She's not the kind of person who would try to take everything over. We should give her a chance."

"But you two don't get it. The more people we get involved, the more we'll have wanting to take charge. How many teachers have you known who actually *don't* try to take something over?"

"A lot," Lauren replied.

"Well, not me."

"Jordan, look," Brett said, lowering his voice. "Here's the deal. We're stuck. If we don't get some help, nothing is going to happen. You know what I'm saying?"

Jordan sat back in his chair and stared at the tip of his thumbnail, biting his lower lip as he thought. He knew what they were saying made perfect sense; he was just too stubborn to admit it.

"Fine. Whatever," he eventually replied. "As long as she doesn't butt in where she doesn't belong."

"Good," Lauren said, picking up her book. "I've got her next period, so if it's okay with you guys, I'll ask her if we can see her after school for a little bit. Meet me outside her room."

Brett wouldn't say it, at least not in front of Lauren, but he was also a little hesitant to get Mrs. Savelle involved. What if she *did* try to take over? What if she tried to take all the credit for all the work? What if — and this is what terrified him the most — what if she tried to make it a *learning experience*? That would definitely kill it in its tracks. But it was a chance he knew they couldn't afford *not* to take.

They were desperate, so it was worth the risk of things becoming *educational*.

The Poe Codec

Letter from Dr. John Carter to Edgar Allan Poe
July, 1849

My Dear Friend Edgar,

I hope this letter finds you better than the previous. I trust the laudanum is doing its job with the headaches.

I wish this letter was of glad tidings, but its nature is of a somber tone. I have received as of this morning a letter from one of your contemporaries, a Mr. Rufus Griswold, with whom I know you are quite familiar. The correspondence does so reek of malice towards your person. Although I have no great friendship with him, he seems to have one with me, and he feels it his liberty to indulge me with his feelings towards you. I know you are well aware that his opinion of you rivals that of his feelings towards Southerners in general.

As such, and as your friend, I must make you aware of his plans. Mr. Griswold intends to ensure that your legacy is greatly tarnished and broken. He is most intent upon this venture. I must warn you to be ever so cautious in your dealings with him, for he has only ill intentions towards you.

He has told me quite clearly that he wishes to destroy your reputation as a writer, as a critic, yes, even as a man, in order to avenge the wrongs you have supposedly inflicted upon him.

Do be careful, friend. I fear that he will not be content until he has achieved his aim.

I look forward to seeing you soon, etc.

Your dear friend,

John Carter, M.D.

XSZKGVI 11

Mrs. Savelle stared at the papers on her desk—speechless. A rare occasion.

"Do you think you could help us?" Lauren asked.

"Wow. I thought you were reading a good book or something simple. I had no idea it would be something like this."

"You think it might be real?" Jordan asked.

"I'm not for sure, but even if it isn't, it's one of the most intriguing projects I've ever encountered. Tell me what I can do to help." Mrs. Savelle had a gift of making even the simplest statement seem profound, or more like something from a cliché poetry book.

When Brett's eyes met Jordan's, he could tell Jordan had the same thought.

"Well, we know with summer vacation coming and all, you're probably going to be busy, so we'd like to be able to get with you when we have a question we can't figure out," Brett said. "Is that okay?"

Mrs. Savelle understood the hint for her involvement to be limited.

"Okay. Any way I can help, just let me know. Since school's almost out for the year, you can contact me through my home email address rather than my school, although I still check both during summer break. How far have you gotten up to now?"

"Well, we figured out that 'The Raven' is going to be the main way we decipher the code, but we don't know how. We can't break the second part of the code," Lauren said as she placed her notes on Mrs. Savelle's desk.

"The letter the word the syllable fit as an equation," Mrs. Savelle read aloud. "Do you have a copy of the poem?"

"Sure." Brett gave her the page he had printed online.

"Somehow, the letters, words, and syllables lead to something. Equation. Numbers. Algebra equations? Let me think . . ."

"Algebra? We found the papers rolled up inside an old algebra book," Brett said. "Do you think that might have something to do with it?"

"You mean the book itself?" Lauren asked. "The one you guys found?"

"Do you still have the book?" Mrs. Savelle asked.

"Dr. Laurence has it in the lab at Dad's school. I can have my dad bring it home tonight," Brett replied.

"Bring it to school tomorrow if you can." Mrs. Savelle laid her glasses on the desk. "That book just might be the key to the door."

XSZKGVI 12

"Did you bring the book?" Jordan asked Brett as he opened the glass door of the school library the next day.

"Right here," he said. "Do you think she'll be able to figure it out?"

"I don't know. I still think we should've tried it without her, though."

"Guys. Over here," Lauren said from one of the computers against the wall.

She and Mrs. Savelle had just begun unpacking papers, books, and laptops onto the table.

"I hope you guys don't mind," Mrs. Savelle said. "But I did a little research last night, and I found something that may help us — I mean — you. Remember in class last semester when I said that Poe was really into codes and cryptograms?"

"Yeah," Lauren and Brett said.

"No," Jordan replied.

"Well, he actually wrote an essay on it called 'A Few Words on Secret Writing.' Real original title, huh? Most people have never heard of it. But look at this first page." She laid the stapled pages on the table and pointed to the third paragraph she had already highlighted. "Here's what you found in the first part of the code, only numbers were substituted for letters. Poe said this was the simplest and most common kind of cryptogram. I guess he used that form just to make it easier for the person trying to break it. I'm guessing he must have thought Rufus Griswold wasn't very intelligent. Or maybe he was just trying to play fair. Who knows?

Anyway, here's what he wrote in the essay: 'We say that some pre-concerted order of this kind is necessary, lest the cipher prove too intricate a lock to yield even to its true key.'"

"So it's all going to make sense, at least eventually, right? As long as we follow the clues in order?" Lauren asked.

"That's the way it sounds," Mrs. Savelle replied. "Only it's up to you guys to work it out."

"Now the sentence we translated the other day from French makes sense," Brett said. "*In order is the only way.*"

"So what does the algebra book have to do with it?" Jordan asked.

"That's what I'm getting to next." Mrs. Savelle flipped to another page of the printout. "Here, Brett, read this paragraph to us. The one I highlighted."

He began to read. "*An unusually secure mode of secret intercommunication might be thus devised. Let the parties each furnish themselves with a copy of the same edition of a book – the rarer the edition the better – as also the rarer the book. In the cryptograph, numbers are used altogether and these numbers refer to the locality of letters in the volume. For example – a cipher is received commencing, 121-6-8. The party addressed refers to page 121, and looks at the sixth letter from the left of the page in the eighth line from the top. Whatever letter he there finds is the initial letter of the epistle – and so on. This method is very secure.*"

"So, here's my theory," Mrs. Savelle continued. "Could I see the book you found and the copy of the code, Brett?"

"Sure." Brett carefully removed the book from his backpack and unzipped the plastic bag encasing it. "The pages are falling out, but they're all still there." He handed her the book with a printout of the picture they had seen on the projector the day Jordan discovered it in the lab.

"Okay. I think Poe might have meant for the poem and the algebra book to be used together. Let's try it out. Flip to the poem on the first page of your packet of papers. Jordan, you count the total number of letters in the first line, and Brett, you count the words. And Lauren, you count the syllables, and we'll see what we come up with. If it all works out the way I'm thinking it will, the number of letters in the line of the poem should tell us what page in the algebra book to look at, the number of words should give us which letter from the left margin it is, and the last number should tell us which line to look at. Jordan, read the first line of the poem, would you?"

"Sure," Jordan answered. He placed his finger on the page and began to read. "Once upon a midnight dreary, while I pondered, weak and weary."

They each began their counting assignment.

"I got forty-nine," Brett said.

"Eleven," Jordan added.

"Sixteen," said Lauren.

"Okay. Forty-nine, eleven, sixteen. What does it say, Brett?"

"Hang on a second."

He carefully turned the brown pages that felt like dried leaves. He scanned his finger lightly over the text, which discussed the Greek influence on the study of algebra. Electrifying reading.

"It looks like the first one is a *t*," he said.

Lauren wrote the letter in her notebook.

"Okay, now look at the second line in the poem," Mrs. Savelle said.

"And do the same thing? This'll take forever," Jordan said.

"Yeah, but at least it's easy, you know? It's really sort of fun, actually." Brett placed the book carefully to the side of his laptop. "I mean it's better than balancing equations, right?"

"Seriously. I love equations," Jordan replied.

"You don't even know what they are."

After several minutes of switching back and forth between "The Raven" and the algebra book, they saw the words *the treasure you seek is in the town of the Owenites* cross Lauren's notebook page.

Before the lines could be discussed, Mrs. Savelle's phone vibrated on the table top.

"Oh, guys, I hate to stop, but I've got a faculty meeting to get to. I've got to go. You can do the rest on your own, right?"

"We think so," Brett said.

"Well, be sure to let me know what it means, okay? I wish I didn't have to leave. I guess I'll see you all on Monday." She stuffed her papers into her bag and walked towards the library doors. "Have a good weekend. And get some sleep, you hear?"

"You guys want to figure out what Owenites are, or stop and do it later?" Lauren asked.

"What do you think?" Brett replied, looking directly into her eyes, this time not looking away, holding her gaze in his.

There was definitely a first time for everything.

XSZKGVI 13

On a remote computer, under the bluish glow of the monitor, fingers methodically pressed keys with determined intent. Slowly, eyes scanned the message once more to verify its accuracy.

It was simple: *V xabj nyy nobhg gur cbr pbqrc. Qb lbh jnag gb gnyx?*

The hand moved the arrow to the send button. A finger hovered over the mouse, hesitant, as if in contemplation, considering the gravity of what it was about to do. There would be no retreat, no turning back, no do-over.

Finally, with a firm tap, the finger pressed, the arrow dropped, and the message disappeared into the outbox.

The eyes patiently waited for a response. The bait was cast. Now the calm wait for the fish to swallow the hook.

A simple substitution code. Split the alphabet and place one half on top of the other. *V* becomes *I*, *X* becomes *K,* and so on until the words *I know all about the poe codec do you want to talk* are neatly coded for the recipient to decode. Not a challenge for this one.

At the other end of the fiber optic wires, cable modems, and wireless signals, Brett smiled. He remembered how Jordan was fixated on making everything a game. Ask Jordan where something was, and he would only give you a hint. *You're getting warmer. You're getting colder. Now you're red hot.* He assumed Jordan must be either bored or avoiding homework. More than likely both. So he clicked the *reply* icon and began typing.

In a few seconds, across the network of wires and routers, a red number one appeared next to the email icon on the other computer. A message in the inbox.

The finger moved the mouse to open the message. In the subject box appeared the words *No need to talk. I'll be the rich guy in the land of the Owenites soon enough. See you at school if you remember to get up.* The mouth smiled.

Then the finger touched the power off button on the monitor and receded into the darkness.

MICHAEL CRANDELL

Letter to Arthur Amsel from Edgar Allan Poe
August, 1849

My Dear Arthur,

How good it was to have received news from you. Your letter was a most welcome gift, as I have anticipated eagerly word of the accommodations. All seems well.

I plan to leave New York near the middle of October. I have discussed the fine details of the venture. I feel my new journal The Stylus will fill the need of a nation starved for wholesome literary nourishment. I intend to stop in Baltimore for a few days to see an old friend, after which I shall begin my journey westward.

I am indeed greatly indebted to Mr. Owen's invitation to live in such an academically and intellectually stimulating community as New Harmony. A utopia! How I long for those days when I shall sit beneath the shade along the bank of the Wabash River, penning all the thousand images and stories alive in my imagination. It shall be a much welcome life.

Muddie thinks it to be exactly what I need. With Virginia gone (how I still miss her so), and no hope, nor desire to remain on the coast, why should I be content with the table scraps of the publishers here? They have no idea of talent, of artistic beauty, of genius. I shall love to converse with the great minds of the world as they unite among the trees of the Indiana woods. I have yet so much to write, that I judge my literary career is just beginning.

As I have forwarded much of my luggage there already, it should be arriving on the coach within the next few weeks. I have also included a lead box with specific instructions I've tucked inside one of my books. Please read the letter, and if you would grant me a great favor as a friend, honor the request I've made as to its handling.

I received the geological maps and the town plans you sent earlier this year. I will inform you of the purposes I have for them when I arrive, as well as the loom card I sent you in the spring.

The descriptions I have read of the old Indiana Territory, of the swift Ohio River, the tranquil Wabash, make me long to be there all the more. I hope to produce enough profit from The Stylus to support myself indefinitely, as I plan to make New Harmony my home permanently, and at the present, see no reason why I should live otherwise.

I will see you in the latter days of October, friend. I bid you warmest regards until then.

Your friend,

E. A. Poe

XSZKGVI 14

"Okay. Good one. Which one of you was it?" Brett asked as he pressed the combination keypad on his locker at school the next morning while sluggish and puffy-eyed students drifted past them in the hall, oblivious to their conversation.

"Was what?" Jordan asked.

"So was it you, then?" Brett looked at Lauren.

"What are you talking about?" she asked.

"That code thing. It was easy to break. All you did was use the example from that Poe essay."

"I seriously have no idea what you're talking about," Jordan said.

"The email. Last night. The one in code. The one that said *I know all about the Poe Codec. Do you want to talk*? Pretty lame, actually." It had jumped out at Brett the minute he'd seen it, and he had promised himself to talk to Jordan and Lauren the next day.

"I didn't send it," Jordan said.

"I didn't either," Lauren added.

"So you're telling me neither one of you sent that email. For real?"

"Why would we send you some stupid email when we see you every day?" Jordan asked.

"So you're saying you got an email about the Poe Codec?" Lauren asked.

"Last night."

"And what did it say again?" she asked.

"It was in code. I thought it was one of you two, so I just used that code in Poe's Secret Writing essay, you know, where he talks about taking the alphabet and splitting it in half and putting half of the letters on top of the others. And when I saw what the message said, I just figured it was one of you two."

"Did you reply to it?" Jordan asked.

"Sort of."

"What do you mean 'sort of'?" Jordan asked sarcastically. "How do you 'sort of' reply to an email?"

"What did you say?" Lauren asked as she stepped closer to Brett.

"I said that I'd see you in the town of the Owenites."

"Are you kidding me?" Jordan exclaimed. "How can you be so stupid?"

"Shut up, okay? I said I thought it was one of you two, so back off. It's not my fault." Brett could feel the blood rushing up his neck and into his cheeks.

"Jordan, he didn't know. I would've probably thought the same thing if I'd gotten the email," Lauren said. "So how could someone else know what we're doing other than Mrs. Savelle, Dr. Laurence, and Brett's dad?"

"Why did you mention the Owenites?" Jordan demanded. "I mean, that was just stupid."

"Look, are you deaf? I said I thought it was you two, okay?" Brett moved toward Jordan till their faces were only inches apart. "How many times do I have to say it?"

"Back up," Jordan said. "I mean it."

"Guys, it's okay," Lauren intervened before punches were thrown. "It's the last week of school. We'll have more time when we get out. Are you two going to be okay, I mean, you're not going to start pounding each other right here in the hallway, are you?"

"Ask him," Brett said as he crossed his arms and leaned against the locker, easing the tension a degree but still maintaining his defense and his stare at Jordan.

Both boys continued to glare at each other. Neither was willing to concede any ground, admit any fault. Until Brett suddenly sneezed — and with it, passed a short, but amplified, burst of gas.

And both burst out in uncontrollable laughter.

"I'm fine," Brett said, his face red from embarrassment and laughing.

"Yeah. It's all good," said Jordan, wiping a tear from his eye.

Lauren turned and left for her locker, pretending to be disgusted, while Brett and Jordan continued to try to stifle their laughs.

Brett admitted it was a stupid mistake — honest, but stupid. He didn't know.

The treasure you seek is in the town of the Owenites, the Eden of Reason of our Age. The rest of the message they had decoded yesterday after Mrs. Savelle left for her faculty meeting. It was relatively simple, following the consistent pattern of letters, words, and syllables in the line of Poe's poem *The Raven*.

For example, line thirty-two in the poem, *Soon again I heard a tapping somewhat louder than before,* contained forty-seven letters, ten words, and fifteen syllables. When cross-referenced with the algebra book, forty-seven told them which page in the book to turn to, ten was the number of letters from the left margin of the page, and fifteen directed them to which line. They simply followed this order and found the three numbers led them to the letter *o*. And the pattern continued.

letters ~ words ~ syllables

47-10-15 Soon again I heard a tapping somewhat louder than before.
49-11-16 Surely, said I surely that is something at my window lattice
46-11-15 Let me see then what thereat is and this mystery explore
45-11-15 Let my heart be still a moment and this mystery explore
24-6-7 'Tis the wind and nothing more

52-13-17 Open here I flung the shutter when with many a flirt and flutt
49-12-15 In there stepped a stately Raven of the saintly days of yore
53-13-16 Not the least obeisance made he not a minute stopped or stayed
→ 3 syllables

OWENITES

— Robert Owen
— New Harmony → Indiana

The treasure you seek is in the town of the Owenites

Town of the Owenites. At first, the three thought Owenites were a type of fossil or geological material, and began searching online for towns famous for fossil finds, but when Jordan suggested they look up *Owenite,* they found that *these* were actually members of a community, and the town was closer than they would have ever imagined.

The Owenites were the followers of Robert Owen, a Welsh factory owner whose ambition was to create a perfect community, a utopia. He bought a small community in southern Indiana named Harmonie from George Rapp, the leader of a religious group known as the Harmonists. Owen changed the name of the community to New Harmony in 1824 and invited several scientists, philosophers, educators, writers, and artists to establish their permanent residence in the community and perfect their professions freely.

Because his cousin Vernon lived there, Brett was familiar with the general layout of the town, although he knew that a visit to New Harmony would also require a visit with Vernon. Possibly even a stay.

Unfortunately.

Vernon. From his earliest memories, Brett loathed the annual summer visitation, which historically annihilated two full weeks of his vacation—fourteen days of the roughly eighty-two in the calendar allocated to pure, undefiled academic freedom. Vernon and Brett shared an involuntary bond in that they were born only two weeks apart (Vernon on June 27 and Brett on July 11). So both their mothers (who were also sisters) began the tradition of the boys spending these weeks together each summer and co-celebrating their birthdays on the Fourth of July, alternating each year between Indianapolis and New Harmony. After Brett's mother died, his Aunt Sophia was even more adamant that the tradition continue, an insistence Brett knew was welcome to his father, since it ensured him of two weeks of uninterrupted work and relative freedom every other year.

Vernon abhorred the outside, and as a result, when Brett visited New Harmony, he typically played by himself somewhere in the yard and surrounding wooded areas, while Vernon sat on the front porch whining about the heat, the bugs, the pollen, the boredom.

(Vernon's mother insisted in Brett's hearing that Vernon do something outside with his cousin, explaining that since Brett lived in Indianapolis, he might want to experience outdoor life a bit more than the opportunities he possibly received at home. But the porch was typically as far as Vernon delved into nature.)

As Brett grew older and could venture further from the house, he began to explore the old town, the remnants of the attempt at an American utopia, to discover its secrets, its untold tales, nearly always on his own.

Gratefully on his own.

It was always nothing less than absolute torture to force himself to interact with Vernon, but on this trip, the timing and location were perfect. When Lauren, Jordan, and he finished decoding the remainder of the *Poe Codec*, it would be close to the end of June, time for his annual birthday rendezvous with Vernon. And it just so happened that this year it was in New Harmony. For once in his life, Brett actually found himself somewhat looking forward to the trip. Somewhat.

But he had always enjoyed the drive there. Interstate 69 reduced the car ride to just over three hours, but he and his father still preferred the old route, exiting I-69 in Bloomington onto Highway 37, which wound north to south through nearly the entire Hoosier National Forest, before eventually merging with Highway 66, their favorite section of the trip, as the two lane road traced the northern bank of the Ohio River. Just about the only thing other than missing his mother they shared in common.

Getting to New Harmony was not the problem. For him. But Jordan and Lauren. That was the issue, the one he would address when the time came. Somehow. But first things first.

Like the email. Where had it come from? Who had sent it? Why?

Who else would even care that three middle-school kids were playing an intriguing puzzle game that in all likelihood wasn't even real?

Brett intended to get answers that night.

XSZKGVI 15

Later, back at his computer, Brett opened the email again. He clicked the reply button as well as the bcc:, typing Lauren's and Jordan's email addresses in the box.

The cursor flashed, eager to receive input. He felt for the small bumps on the *f* and *j* keys with his index fingers and placed the rest of his fingers on home row. He inhaled. Exhaled.

And typed *yes*.

Then clicked *send*.

And he waited.

Elsewhere in town, the eyes saw the small icon appear in the corner of the screen, announcing the incoming message. The hand moved the arrow to the box and clicked. The message simply said *yes*. The hand moved the arrow again, to the *reply* button, and clicked. The fingers typed letters into the *instant message* window, the old-school method of digital communication, but still quick, and still anonymous. The hand pressed *send*.

And then the mouth smiled.

XSZKGVI 16

Brett: Who r u???

Unknown: First of all, none of this texting stupidity. If you want to talk, do it right.

Brett: Fine. So why did you send your first message in code?

Unknown: To get your attention, a strategy I assume worked. I'll get to the point. We know what you're doing and what you're looking for.

Brett: How?

Unknown: That's not the issue. What matters is how badly you want to find it.

Brett: Find what?

Unknown: Keep this up, and I log off. Then that huge question mark will be in your head for the rest of your life. No games here. You know what I'm talking about. What Poe left Rufus Griswold. *The treasure that you seek.* Right?

Brett: So what do you want from me?

Unknown: A partnership.

Brett: What kind?

Unknown: The silent kind. The kind where you forward the rest of the code to us, and we disappear.

Brett: What do you mean?

Unknown: Just what I said. Attach everything you've done to the email you received the other day, and life returns to normal. Simple as that.

Brett: It's ours. We found it, and we've worked too hard to get this far just to give it away.

Unknown: Like finders keepers, right? I get it. Just understand that this is the last time we make this offer. Send us what you have and we disappear. We will have never existed.

Brett: What if I say no?

Unknown: Then I'll write the ending to the story myself. Do you remember "The Cask of Amontillado"?

Brett: Sort of.

Unknown: My apologies. I forgot. Lauren is the Poe expert among the three of you.

Brett: How do you know about Lauren?

Unknown: What don't we know? Anyway, in "The Cask," the narrator sets a trap for his victim. He lures Fortunato into the catacombs by using his arrogance against him. Fortunato's pride kills him. Don't be stupid. You wouldn't want anything bad like that to happen to you and your friends because you didn't listen. Last chance. Refuse this request and I promise you, we will use you against yourself. Make the right choice here. Adieu.

Brett: What do you mean?

Unknown: (No response.)

Brett: WHO ARE YOU??? HOW DO YOU KNOW WHO I AM???

Unknown: (No response.)

XSZLGVI 17

"Use you against yourself?" Fear fringed Lauren's words. "What's that supposed to mean?" she said as she closed her locker door.

"No idea," Brett said. "All I know is that whoever they are, they're serious, and they know a lot about us. It's like they're watching us somehow."

"How?" Jordan asked.

"I don't get it," Brett replied. "They know things only we should know. Like how you're the one who knows everything about Poe, Lauren. How would anybody else know something like that? This whole thing isn't right. "

"Whoever they are, it sounds like they know about New Harmony. But how would they know about *that*?" Jordan said.

"We've got to tell someone," Lauren added.

"Who?" Brett asked. "Who can we tell?"

"Your dad. Dr. Laurence. Mrs. Savelle. Somebody."

"Or — what if it's one of them?" Jordan said.

"Come on, Jordan. Not the whole conspiracy thing."

"Well, what if it *is* one of them?" Lauren asked. "Think about it. Who else would know what we're doing?"

"Seriously? Not you, too, Lauren," Brett said, throwing his head back and sighing.

"Okay, so maybe you're right," she said to Brett. "But it just doesn't make sense. Why us?"

"I know I'm right, and I can promise you, whoever they are, they aren't playing around," Brett said. "I mean, they didn't come right out and threaten me, but they got about as close as they could without saying it. I don't know who these people are, but they sound serious . . . and dangerous. I can tell you this much—I'm not going to reply to anymore emails. From anybody. But the upside to all this is that they're only emailing me. So far you guys are okay."

"Define 'okay'," Jordan replied. "They mentioned our names, too."

"Don't worry," Brett said, lifting the door handle lightly as he shut the door to avoid shifting the combination lock he always kept preset. "I won't let anything happen to you. I promise."

"I feel safer already, then," Jordan answered. "Thanks, bodyguard."

Brett glanced at Lauren. She smiled.

"Like I said, don't worry," Brett repeated.

Little did he know things would not be so simple.

XSZKGVI 18

Brett gazed at the two flashing dots on the nightstand clock, watching them count down more seconds of sleep slipping from him. He tried willing himself to sleep, tried to empty his mind of all the patterns, the encoding, the decoding jostling inside, but the more he resisted the puzzle, the more sleep evaded him. Too much consumed his thoughts. Tomorrow—or today—was the last day of school.

Finally.

The Last Day. Locker cleanout, morning periods of mindless movies released two decades ago, outside to Eighth Grade Day, an afternoon of signing yearbooks, playing basketball, hanging out, doing anything but sitting inside. The first official act ushering in the summer.

But thinking about all these did nothing to help him sleep.

His father being nearly non-existent didn't help, either. Physically present, yes, but consciously in another world, thinking things Brett would never understand, would never care to understand. Brett loved his father—or at least he knew he should, and he knew his father loved him—or at least he should, but the distance was there. And both, apparently, were content to keep it.

During the few instances when they did speak, Brett would look into his father's eyes and see them elsewhere, looking beyond him, maybe for the next major research project, or the next great idea for one of the ten or so journals he submitted articles to. Maybe it was simply boredom, or disappointment. Or that gray, clouded intuition that you never quite became who you envisioned yourself becoming.

Brett had heard it called a *midlife crisis*. He had no concept of what it was, nor did he care. Leave that to the counselors.

But he knew the real reason, as much as he tried to pretend, tried to keep heaping the blame onto his father. It was his mother.

And they both had let the crack between them become a chasm, and both felt the embarrassment that it had become so wide, so apparently irreconcilable that the only way they could co-exist was to deny the obvious and accept the illusion that this was just the way the other wanted it to be. The way it was supposed to be.

At the same time he resented his father's absence, Brett held a sinking fear that he would never return. Traveling back and forth from the University on the busy Interstate, his father could have an accident. He could get kidnapped, shot, hijacked—he could die. But what terrified Brett was not so much the grief he would feel at his father's death, the void Brett would feel in missing him—he would—but it was that he would be forced into more responsibility, that he would have to step into the role now delegated to him. The provider. The One Depended Upon.

He would have to grow up—but as an orphan.

Brett hated himself for being so narcissistic, so self-centered. He often wondered if he was alone in such thinking, if only crazy people had such thoughts. Grief at a parent's death, not from loss of someone you love—like the grief he felt for his mother—but from the realization of how the death will change your life.

That haunted him most.

It was too much to resolve in one sleepless night.

Then there was the Codec. At times he wished he and Jordan had never taken a single step into the Hemington building, never found the book, never seen the parchments rolled inside. In the days since then, this detective role-play had consumed nearly all of his life, siphoned away his concentration, his grades, now even his sleep. It had been only days, but it felt like the emotional weight of months seemed to press down on him, exhausting him mentally, draining his mind of thoughts beyond numbers and letters and symbols and patterns.

And he was nearly at his end with the secrecy, the constant whispering, the endless looking over the shoulder for people not there. It had become his life — and he felt controlled by it. By what?

A game.

Perhaps this was how a person with an addiction feels. Trying to run away from it, avoiding it, not focusing on it, but it keeps coming back, always coming back. Again. And again.

And again.

Then there was Lauren.

What focus remained from the Poe Codec, Brett had expended on her, the way she tucked her red hair behind her ear when she was concentrating, how she twisted her wrist to straighten her bracelet with the dangling silver heart. He loved everything about her. Her voice. Her laugh. How she slid the cross on her necklace from side to side when she was nervous.

He felt his sanity slowly slipping from his grasp.

He had come close to telling her how he felt last week. They were sitting at a library table across from each other. He moved his leg, bumping something — a table leg — or hers. But it didn't move like most people's if bumped accidentally. He felt the blood flush his neck, crawl to his cheeks and ears. His attention abruptly shifted from the Poe Codec to the leg — whichever kind it was. Then it moved.

And he knew.

He glanced up quickly, his eyes meeting hers. Then just as quickly, she glanced back down to the paper. But for that fraction of a second, they were looking at each other. Eye to eye. Brett could feel his pulse

pounding in his neck and felt the blood rush again to his ears. His cheeks burned. Did she see him the same way? Did she feel the same?

It was enough to give anyone insomnia.

Then there were the mysterious emails.

His stomach fluttered every time he thought of that business about "The Cask of Amontillado." A joke or a threat? He still suspected Jordan or Lauren of being behind it—but they both denied it—emphatically. He tried to convince himself it was a joke, but the more he denied its gravity, the more aware he was of it. How could they know so much about him, about what they were doing?

Who were they?

Brett mentally replayed the online conversation over and over. How serious was the person who wrote him? How serious was the threat?

He was terrified of the unknown. Sensibly, he should tell his father, the police, the FBI—anybody—but what then? If people knew about the Poe Codec, and if it was in fact legitimate, all their notes, the letter and the code papers, the algebra book, all of it would be confiscated as evidence, likely indefinitely. It would all be over, and perhaps someone older, more qualified (like one of his dad's and Dr. Laurence's ancient colleagues) would get the credit for discovering Edgar Allan Poe's unknown fortune. They would publish a bestseller about it, sell the movie rights, and make countless talk show appearances while Brett, Jordan, and Lauren stood on the sidelines. Watching.

But at least alive.

Was the purpose of life, then, merely to preserve it?

Brett remembered one of the Sundays his mother took him to church the year before she died. The teacher, whose name he had either long forgotten or never really known, was the typical old-lady Sunday School teacher. Gray hair in a style two decades too old, flowery dress, colorful plastic costume jewelry that clinked when she moved her arms to emphasize a point. Someone's grandma. *Everyone's* grandma.

The Bible verse for that day was John 15:13, when Jesus says, "Greater love has no one than this: to lay down one's life for his friends." Brett had long forgotten the point of the lesson, but he remembered the verse because of how bizarre and confusing it sounded, even then as a seven-year-old. Sacrifice. To give up your life to protect someone else's. He loved Lauren and Jordan. He knew he did. And lying in his bed, cocooned from all apparent danger, it was easy to make this resolve, to feel the confidence of courage that if circumstances dictated it, he would do whatever was necessary to protect his friends. No matter the cost. No matter the consequences. No matter what.

He squinted at the clock next to his head and decided. He would go to New Harmony alone, without Jordan and Lauren. Even if by some inconceivable way they could actually manage to get there, he would do whatever it took to keep them from coming along. Even if it cost him their friendship. He would go to New Harmony alone. Even if it cost him his life.

But often courage is strongest when danger is weakest.

As irrational as it appeared, Brett was now more than ever committed to solving the Poe Codec. But the entire project was *their* discovery, *their* work, and it was *their* right to claim it. Was he merely attempting to play the fictional action movie hero, all-out, full-throttle—with no regard for his personal safety? Delusionally believing that when the intensity rose too high, became too out of control, someone would yell "cut" from the side and it all would be over? Maybe. But he knew if he was honest with himself, he was terrified. However, finding the treasure, or the end, or whatever, might change things. Possibly everything.

XSZKGVI 19

All the pieces were finally in place. They had done it.

Finally.

But what should have been a celebration was a nightmare.

It was like Ralphie in the movie *A Christmas Story* when he finally gets the Red Ryder BB gun, only to nearly shoot his eye out. It wasn't what Brett thought it would be. In fact, when he should have been celebrating, he was nauseated, sick with the feeling that it was too easy. There had to be a catch somewhere, a hidden clause, some fine print he failed to read.

The remainder of the code eventually fell into place, but only after Jordan—amazingly of the four (including Mrs. Savelle)—made the mental leap from concrete thinking to the abstract.

After they decoded *The treasure you seek is in the town of the Owenites,* only phrases began to emerge, like *hideous heart, Spanish wine,* and *kingdom by the sea,* until all the remaining lines of the poem *The Raven* were used. Lauren immediately recognized that the phrases referred to Poe's two short stories "The Tell-Tale Heart" and "The Cask of Amontillado," as well as his poem "Annabel Lee." But they had exhausted the lines in *The Raven*. All that remained on the original code sheet were the rows upon rows of numbers adjacent to the three rows of letters that led them to the key to connecting the algebra book with the letters, words, and syllables of the poem. Nothing else provided a bridge to anything.

Without announcing to anyone what he was doing, Jordan quietly, almost secretively, opened the browser on the computer in the back of Mrs. Savelle's room and found an online copy of Poe's "The Tell-Tale Heart." Obviously, the letter, word, syllable sequence would not work, as there was no way to determine a page number or line ending, since most online texts rarely have consistent page breaks within documents. Jordan remembered Lauren had mentioned that Poe's short stories were first published in newspaper or gazette format, so even the original typesetting would change depending upon the size and font preference of the typesetter.

As Jordan scanned his copy of the original code sheet, he noticed that ninety-nine was the highest number, which meant that if this were another form of a substitution code—and more than likely it was—letters would have more than one representative number. In other words, a letter could have up to four different numbers substituted for it. But as he traced his finger along the rows and columns of numbers, that magical, most-used letter in the alphabet never stood out. He could not find any number used more often than any other. No representative for *e*.

So what would every story and poem have in common? he asked himself, tapping the top of the computer mouse.

A beginning and an end.

Starting with the first row of numbers on the code sheet and going across, Jordan began counting the number of letters from the beginning of the story. The first number on the code sheet was one. The first letter of the story "The Tell-Tale Heart" was *t*. The second number was twenty-three; the twenty-third letter of the story was *a*.

When Brett noticed Jordan working, he asked him what he was doing.

"Cracking the Poe Codec," he said with a smirk. "You about ready to help me?"

It was a boring and tedious process, but they eventually decoded all the numbers, resulting in a series of specific directions, which they assumed referred to New Harmony, *the town of the Owenites.*

And created an entirely new set of problems to solve.

Even beyond the Poe Codec.

The line in the email he received the other night was branded into Brett's memory. *Refuse this request and I promise you, I will use you against yourself.* How could he know the true resolve of the threat? He didn't, and that was the true test of courage, to act in the midst of the unknown, to do without knowing the outcome. His pledge to protect his friends at all costs—to "lay down his life" if necessary—suddenly consumed his consciousness, bringing him nearly to tears. He loved them—more than they would ever know or he would ever tell them—and he knew what he had to do. Even if it cost him their love.

He couldn't tell them that he was terrified beyond any fragment of logic to go to New Harmony, that he knew that *they* would be there, whoever they were sending the emails, the enigma that seemed to have the ability to extract every thought in his head, to hear every word, see every action. *They* would be waiting for him, somehow, somewhere, ready to execute any measures necessary to obtain what the Poe Codec revealed.

Whatever it is.

He loved them both. Jordan was like a brother—no, he *was* a brother—although Brett would never tell him that, couldn't tell him. And Lauren. He just loved her.

He could never deliberately lead them into a potentially threatening situation. He could not let anything happen to either one of them, at any price.

Which was precisely why he had to ensure that he would go alone.

He detested creating the little dramatic episode in order to sever his ties to Jordan and Lauren, opening a chasm he hoped would only be temporary. It horrified him to think that he would possibly demolish a bridge which might never be reconstructed. But he knew no other way. To protect the two he loved, he had to annihilate that love. The rationale was illogical, perhaps even wrong, but he knew the thought of either one of them being led into any type of danger — not to mention one he intentionally brought them into — drew him into extreme action.

"It's not fair, and you know it," Jordan said, pointing his finger in Brett's face after he gave his friends the news that he was going to New Harmony alone. "We worked our butts off just as much as you did! We should get to go too!"

"Like I said. Find a way to get there on your own," Brett said calmly.

"It figures." Jordan spat the words at Brett. "You just wanted everything for yourself all along, and you just used us to get it. Why am I not surprised?"

"Brett, it really isn't fair that you're the only one who gets to go. Jordan does have a point," Lauren said, trying to relax the building tension between the boys. "We *did* help, too. I mean, the money would be nice, but I'm more interested in seeing if it's all really true. If anything, we should get to find out, right?"

"So you're on his side, then, right? Do you two think that's what this is all about? The money or whatever it is? Are you kidding me?"

"Brett, wait. You —"

"No, that's okay, Lauren. I get it. I should have known."

Brett threw the folder onto the floor, the collection of nearly a month of his life, all the notes he had taken on the Codec, all scattered across the tile. He followed the folder with the algebra book, its spine splitting, spreading loose pages which intermixed with the notes already on the library floor.

"There you go," he said, calmly, coldly. "A little souvenir for the two of you. I've got my own copies. I'll let you know how it goes. See you around."

Brett walked through the library doors refusing to turn around, fighting the urge for one last look at the two, resisting the temptation to tell them the truth.

That he didn't mean a word of it.

Even as he pulled his bike from the tubular steel rack, he felt the pang of deception drive even deeper. He knew traveling to New Harmony packing all the materials of the Poe Codec might be more than risky.

It might be lethal.

So before he arrived at the library, Brett had taken pictures of all the documents and saved them on his phone. Every note, every scribble, every direction. Safe. Secure.

If only life was that efficient.

Touch a button and everything perfectly, cleanly, slips exactly into its proper space. No complications. But lately, his life had become a computer with a virus, or a phone dropped into water, everything scrambled, chaotic, nothing fitting where it should.

An entire system about to crash.

As he pedaled his bike home, he felt the tears come. *Don't,* he thought, almost aloud. *You don't cry.* The harder he fought them, the stronger the tears came. He knew he could mend things with Jordan; they had endured many more incidents than this. Jordan would pout for a few days, speak his mind, and gradually life would return to normal between them.

But Lauren. Brett knew that he had crushed any hope of a future with her, that he would be helpless to undo what he had done to her.

It was over before it ever started.

This thing, this *Poe Codec*, began as an interesting game, an intriguing puzzle which might hold a gratifying prize at the end, but now, as systematic as its code, it was consuming him, overtaking him, letter by letter.

It was destroying him. And his connection with everything and everyone around him.

He wanted it over. All of it. Money or not, real or not, he wanted it to end. No amount of reward could reimburse him for what he had lost in the last few weeks.

His only focus was to finish what they'd started.

And walk away from it. Permanently.

Brett realized he would be alone until the end. Getting Lauren and Jordan out of it had been difficult. One of the most difficult actions he had ever had to take. But he knew there was really no other way, no other path to circumvent the obvious threat to them. He also realized the most exacting times had yet to begin. The storm was forming on the horizon. The worst was approaching, and he dreaded it.

He knew he had to make the call to his cousin to let him know he would be there in a few days, another ridiculous tradition their mothers began and Brett's aunt still continued. It was cute when they were three. Not so cute at fourteen.

Two weeks with Vernon.

He dreaded that nearly worst of all.

PART II:
NEW HARMONY

CHAP73R 1

Highway 69 curved through the center of Posey County, corn and soybean fields hedging the road on either side, parallel rows of endless green passing the car window. While the trip lacked breathtaking scenery, it compensated Brett with relaxation, the kind born not from boredom, but from a slower stride, a more tranquil atmosphere. The essence of New Harmony.

Fields yielded abruptly to trees after the turn from the highway onto Maple Hill Road, one of the main arteries leading to the town's heart. The smooth asphalt, well-maintained, curved downhill through a corridor of trees whose interwoven tops formed a portal to another place in a seemingly different time, as if Brett and his dad were traveling through the wardrobe into Narnia. To the left, the Maple Hill Cemetery ascended the hill, a welcoming testament to the town's history and its permanence, a place where names engraved on the markers mirrored those on the mailboxes.

Maple Hill Road renamed itself Main Street as it passed the labyrinth, the maze of shrubbery planted as a reconstruction of the original settlers' intention for it to serve as a place of prayer and contemplation; they likely never foresaw the sanctuary transforming into a scenic tourist stop.

Brett's cousin Vernon lived near Murphy Park in one of the newer homes designed to look antiquated, and thus aesthetically harmonize with the surrounding structures, a concept fundamental to the style of most of the town's buildings. Yet despite the exterior's archaic design, the house's interior was ultra-contemporary, radiating a modern ambiance that greatly appealed to Brett.

His uncle Madison, Vernon's father, was the Chief Engineer of the NASA division of a prominent firm in Chicago, a company that contracted mainly for satellite placement and deep space explorer modules. Despite earning a substantial salary for his expertise, his uncle never lost his fascination with innovative technology.

He was an electronic gadget junkie.

He was nearly always the first to obtain the latest device, notably the experimental prototypes still in development, years from the commercial market. He also enjoyed modifying common electronic devices to enhance their productivity or alter their function. He once modified one of Vernon's game systems to allow it to play the experimental training programs his company used in the Space Program. But like Brett's father, Madison was often away; only he worked in Chicago during the week, commuting home on weekends—perhaps the reason why Brett's aunt Sophia went to great lengths to make his stays memorable. Brett loved the extra attention, the great meals, and the kettle corn.

Definitely the kettle corn.

His aunt popped it in an old iron kettle she had purchased years ago in one of the antique stores on Main Street, adding the sugar as the popcorn kernels pinged against the inside and eventually spilled over the top and onto the countertop like yellow lava.

So it was no surprise when she exclaimed "Brett!" as she opened the large oak door of the entry to Brett and his father. "Come here! Let me see you. My gosh, you've grown about a foot since last Christmas! I just popped a batch of kettle corn this morning. Sit down and tell me what you've been up to."

His father embraced his sister-in-law, and the two talked to each other all through lunch until it was time for Jeff to begin the trip back to Indianapolis.

And for Brett to begin taking on the kettle corn.

CHAP73R 2

Later, after his father had headed home, Brett was unpacking his duffel bag when Vernon stepped into the doorway of the guest bedroom, blurting as he always did, as if Brett were thirty feet away, "So what do you want to do?"

Brett jumped. Vernon seemed completely oblivious to any category of social skills or rules, or any kind of etiquette in general. He was always yelling at people with their backs turned. Walking into people when walking with them side by side. Or like last summer when Brett was helping mow the lawn and almost severed his foot when it nearly slid under the lawnmower after he fell backward because Vernon pushed him on the shoulder to gain his attention. Vernon was illiterate where etiquette was concerned, something which Brett could never understand, considering how refined his aunt and uncle were, and how often Vernon attended elaborate dinners in Chicago and other social events with his parents. He had exposure to proper social interaction; it just seemed to have never sunk in.

Perhaps that was why Vernon was the way he was—his family was so wealthy, etiquette was optional, an accessory, not a mandate. At least to him.

Vernon had the perpetual look of sleeping in his clothes—and just getting out of bed. He was close to Brett's height, about average for a boy going into high school, but slightly overweight. His blonde hair never seemed to be combed or brushed, but it was always neatly cut, out of insistence from his mother that he was "not going to run around looking like he just crawled out of a dumpster." Vernon rarely ran around at all anyway.

Brett picked up the underwear and socks he dropped at Vernon's explosive entry.

"Seriously, Vernon, I wish you wouldn't do that."

"What?"

"Nothing. Never mind."

"Mom said since you're the guest, I'm supposed to let you pick out the stuff to do. So, pick."

Vernon had the gift of hospitality, of making someone feel really welcome.

"Well, maybe we can play your game system for a little while."

"Can't. Mom said I'm on it too much, so I'm grounded from it."

Great. One of the only things he and Vernon had in common, one of the only things on the planet they could actually do *together*, and he gets himself banned from it.

Thanks, cousin.

Then Brett remembered Vernon's older brother Kyle, a junior at Wabash College, was staying on campus to take summer courses, which meant Brett had free use of his bike, a custom-built mountain bike that weighed less than ten pounds total. A sweet ride. And Brett's for two weeks.

"Then maybe we can ride the bikes downtown and see what's playing at the theater."

"Why do you want to go there? They just show plays and crap like that."

"I mean the cinema. The *movie* theater, not the Opera House."

"Okay, but you didn't say that."

"I—yeah, I know. I'm sorry."

Brett learned long ago that it was much easier to just say you're sorry and move forward with your life than to try to debate with Vernon, much less offer any kind of explanation. They were both the same age, and their mothers had been sisters. Still, it constantly amazed Brett that he and his cousin were actually related. They were about as different as two people could be.

It also perplexed Brett that Vernon had lived in New Harmony his entire life and still said the "theater" when he meant Thrall's Opera House, one of the historic buildings constructed when the Rappites founded Harmonie, the original community, in the early 1800s.

Brett had only a moderate interest in history, but he found the town still fascinating. Close to two hundred years old, and several of the buildings just as old, nearly every one containing an interesting story.

But Vernon could care less.

CHAP73R 3

The shade from the branches overhead made the bike ride more enjoyable, and Brett was glad the settlers had sense enough to leave as many trees as they did when clearing the area to establish the town. Shade in southern Indiana summers was almost as valuable as Florida beachfront property, but even with the sun's heat blocked overhead, Vernon continued to complain.

"We should have got one of the golf carts instead of taking these stupid bikes," he whined. "It's too hot out here."

Brett tried to ride his bicycle ahead—not much of a challenge—so he could pretend he didn't hear Vernon.

New Harmony and Indianapolis were nearly polar opposites, as much as two communities could be, especially in how people interacted. In Indy, most people ignored each other when passing, often avoiding eye contact. Here, however, even if people were unfamiliar, most still greeted one another. Yet, despite the friendly aura, visitors still knew they were outsiders. At least that was how Brett always felt when he visited. Everything in New Harmony was so permanent, so always there.

Most of the residents could trace their ancestry to the first group of Rappites who floated down the Ohio River and up the Wabash River in flatboats to settle and establish a utopian community in the old Indiana Territory. Even when people remodeled or renovated an old building, a house or a business, they never really attempted to change it, but seemed to focus their effort into *restoring* it, bringing it back to its beginnings. Or at least close to it.

Brett coasted the bike to a stop in front of the theater—the cinema—and waited for Vernon to catch up. Even coasting was laborious for him. Brett speculated that this was Vernon's only ride since his visit last year.

A lady in running clothes and headphones approached as Vernon panted and wheezed his bike to the curb.

"Hi, Vernon. Hello, Brett," she said as she passed, her arms pumping in stride with her steps.

"Hi," Brett replied with no idea who she was.

"Hey, Vernon, who was that?"

"Who?"

"The lady that just went by."

"What lady?"

It was then Brett noticed Vernon had been watching his feet nearly the entire time they had been riding, concerned that his shoelaces might snag in the chain and sprocket.

"Never mind," Brett said with a sigh.

That was another trait Brett loved about New Harmony. People knew each other—knew about each other—actually *cared* to know about each other. More than likely the lady was one of his aunt's friends.

And yet still cared enough to know his name.

"You want to come back tonight? The 7:10 movie looks good," Brett asked Vernon's butt, which was elevated approximately two feet from Brett's face as Vernon bent over to triple knot his shoelaces—a sight Brett wanted to avoid burning into his memory.

"Yeah, whatever. Hey, let's go home and get something to eat," Vernon said as he stood up, pulling his shorts back to where they should have been originally.

Brett then heard it, the noise suddenly erupting from Vernon's shorts, sounding like a weed eater motor.

"That was a good one," Vernon said, smiling proudly.

It was definitely going to be a long visit.

A very long visit.

CHAP73R 4

A small compensation for tolerating Vernon for two weeks, as Brett defined it, was that he got his own room, a small break of a few hours from his cousin.

That night after everyone else had gone to bed, Brett took his phone from his duffel bag and pressed the power button, careful not to wake the family. He tapped the small screen until he found the downloaded pictures of the Poe Codec notes, which consisted primarily of what seemed to be directions and descriptions of landmarks in the town. He reviewed them, thinking of how and where and when to begin trying to find what he came for.

But there was Vernon. Not even under the most desperate circumstances would Brett ever contemplate asking for his help, trying to follow the directions of the code while simultaneously attempting to keep him quiet and out of the way. But he could do nothing without Vernon plowing in. Where Brett went, he followed, but as painfully annoying as he was, Vernon was a good guide. He knew the layout of New Harmony and its locations, despite his indifference concerning anything even remotely interesting about the town, so he could assist Brett in finding what he needed—regardless of not knowing exactly how he was helping, or for what.

Brett heard short bursts of buzzes from his duffel bag. His phone. He turned the ringer off earlier so he could still answer texts without waking everyone up. In case Jordan called. Or Lauren.

Just in case.

It was torture. It had been only a few days, but years had seemed to pass, long enough for Brett to nearly forget what she looked like. He missed her to the extent that it actually ached. He understood what Charlie Gordon meant in the story *Flowers for Algernon* when he said what he felt was like "heartburn and getting punched in the chest at the same time."

Brett loved Lauren.

At least he thought he did, if that was what love was supposed to feel like.

The caller I.D. glowed "unknown" as he tapped the answer button on the phone, hoping, praying, *willing* that it would be Lauren calling to tell him that everything was fine, that she understood, that she loved him back.

Who else would call him at one o'clock in the morning?

"Hello?" he asked in a muffled whisper.

No response.

"Hello?" he asked again.

"Hi Brett." The voice sounded garbled, distorted, as if it were underwater.

"Who is this?" he asked.

"You know who. Well, you don't actually know who, but you do know who," the voice replied.

"What?"

"Really, Brett, did you think we'd disappear? Just vanish when you came to town? I would hope you'd give us more credit than that."

"You're the—"

"Yes, we're the . . . don't know what to call us, do you? Well, let's see . . . since we'll be working pretty closely together, how about you just calling us Partner, or maybe just Pat for short."

"How'd you get my cell number?"

"How do I know *anything* about you? It's a puzzle, isn't it? But that's a trade secret. I can't let you peek behind the curtain, now can I? Maybe later. But let's focus on what's important right now, because we've got work to do."

"What do you want?"

"The same thing we did when you were in Indianapolis. That's all."

"I gave that stuff to Lauren and Jordan. Since you know so much about everything, I figured you'd already know that, too."

"So why are you here in New Harmony visiting dear cousin Vernon? Seriously, we both know better. What a pain in the butt. How *do* you put up with him?"

"What do you mean 'here'?"

"Here. Aqui. New Harmony, Indiana. Crossroads of America. Where else?"

Brett felt the blood flush his neck and face. How did they find him? How did they know? He felt sick.

"I mean it. Leave me alone," Brett said, trying to sound intimidating at first, but ending like a terrified child.

"Not a problem. You know what to do to make us disappear. Simple solution. Brett, I know you have more than one copy of the notes. I'll make it easy. There's a newspaper kiosk in front of The Yellow Tavern. You've seen it. The one where you put the money in and unlock the lid. Pay for a paper, put your copies of the directions inside the box, and close it. Then walk away. Don't hang around. Do that, and it's over. All finished. I'll tell you what. We'll give you a portion of the money as compensation for all you've had to go through to help, since *you* were the one who broke the codes. It'll be between you and us. Jordan and Lauren will never have to know. So, what do you say, Brett? Partners? Brett? Are you there? Let's settle this once and for —"

Brett pressed *end* on the phone. They assumed the notes were still on paper, thankfully, and had no knowledge of the pictures on his phone, and as far as he was concerned, what they didn't know, whoever they were, wouldn't hurt them.

CHAP73R 5

"Hey, Vernon, you want to help me with a summer research project?" Brett asked as they rode the bikes downtown after breakfast.

"Why? What'd you do, flunk or something and have to take summer school?"

"No. I'm helping my dad's university with a project they're working on."

Brett hated lying because it was wrong, and because he was terrible at it.

"How much?"

"What do you mean 'how much?'" Brett asked.

"How much you going to pay me?"

"Pay you?"

"You heard me," Vernon replied, licking orange cheese-curl powder from the fingers on his free hand. "What are you going to give me for helping you?"

Brett almost punched him. *Give you? You should be paying me for putting up with your whining, gas-passing rear end for half my summer. I ought to get a salary for it. Or a trophy. Or the Nobel Prize.*

"Okay, I'll buy your popcorn and drink the next time we go to the movies."

"Mom gives me money."

What a jerk.

"All right. Fine. After you help me, I'll do whatever you want to do, and I'll make your mom think I want to do it. That way, she'll think you're being a good host and I'm just thrilled to be following your decisions. Good enough?"

Brett knew how to work Vernon, and he also knew he had just condemned himself. He didn't want to even think about what idiotic, brain-numbing, activities Vernon would have him doing as payback for the rest of his stay.

"Now you're talking. No more letting you pick everything we do. So what do I have to do for this stupid project?"

"Okay. I need some help working out these directions," Brett said, stopping the bike next to a long brick wall that lined the street and taking out his phone. "You know this town way better than I do, so you can sort of be my guide." He looked at the first location on the list, a compilation of names and places from the original code. "So, do you know what the 'Watchman's Chant' is?"

"The what?"

"The 'Watchman's Chant.' You know anything about it?"

"I don't know what in the world you're talking about. This is already boring."

Brett knew he should have never asked for Vernon's help.

"I've got to find it. Who could we ask that would know something about it?"

"How am I supposed to know?"

What do you know, other than how to make everyone around you want to pound your head in?

Brett saw an older woman across the street looking into one of the downtown shop windows.

"I'll be back in a minute," he said.

"Whatever," Vernon replied, dumping his bike on its side to lie on the bench near the street curb.

"Ma'am? Do you know where I can find the 'Watchman's

Chant'?" Brett asked the woman, who turned from the window with a pleasant, grandmotherly smile.

"The 'Watchman's Chant'? The old Rappite quote?"

"I think so."

"Oh, yes. See that boy over there, the one lying on that bench? I think that's Sophia's boy. Well, it's right behind him."

The brick wall that lined the sidewalk Brett and Vernon were following contained a small alcove with a brick bench inside. Etched in the concrete wall, which also served as the bench back, were thin letters comprising a quotation. The outset of the final phase of the Poe Codec. The "Watchman's Chant." The beginning of the end.

Leave it to the moron—who actually lived in this town—to be oblivious to everything around him.

Even when it was right in front of him.

Or behind.

CHAP73R 6

"What're you looking at?" Vernon asked condescendingly.

"Get up."

"Whatever. I was here first. You don't own this bench. It's hot out here anyway."

"I said get up. There's something I need to see behind you."

Vernon turned around and looked at the words on the wall.

"It's just that stupid old quote. What's the big deal?"

"That stupid quote is exactly what I'm looking for."

"What's so great about it? It's what the guards from the settlement yelled out at night to keep the people in line. So what?"

Vernon was a living version of the History Channel and didn't even realize it, or could just care less. Because of the town's eminence in American history, local students were required to complete an extensive study of events in New Harmony's past. Vernon had known the "Watchman's Chant" since fourth grade and could recite it verbatim, but had no interest whatsoever in its meaning or its significance or its name. To him, it was the stupid thing they had to memorize for a grade.

During the early nineteenth century, in Harmonie (the first of the two Utopian communities on the town's site), to remind the citizens of their purpose for being there (to create a society founded on perfecting the soul), a night watchman recited this chant every hour so all in the community would hear it: *"Again a day is past, and a step made nearer to our end. Our time runs away, and the joys of heaven are our reward."*

Brett stared at the same words, fixed in concrete on the brick wall. *The Watchman's Chant.* He knew what he had to do. The directions gave another series of numbers, just like the other part of the Codec. At least Poe, or whoever wrote it, was consistent. Brett looked at the list on his phone screen and smiled.

"Vernon, here's where we start. When I tell you a number, count from the beginning of the chant and write the letter it ends on in this notebook."

"What? I'm not doing that. That's stupid. Let's go home."

"Hey, you promised you'd help me, so come on."

"I changed my mind. Do it yourself. I'm going home."

Without warning or the slow build-up that usually preceded losing his patience, Brett detonated. Vernon had finally taken him to the brink. He had fought it initially, tried to contain his rage, but his patience had drained. Evaporated. He stepped toward Vernon until his face was inches from his cousin's, and looked directly into his eyes.

"I've had it with you. You hear me?" Brett hissed through clenched teeth in a low, threatening, near-whisper. "I am sick and tired of your crap. I've put up with you my whole life, and I've had it. I'm going to tell you this one time, so you'd better shut your mouth and listen. Maybe you'll stop acting like an idiot for once when you hear what I've got to say."

Brett unloaded all of it—everything—from the beginning with the algebra book in the old bookstore back home in Indianapolis. It might have been the single most senseless thing he had ever done, even worse than what he had done to Lauren and Jordan, but he no longer cared. He was tired. Tired of all of it. Vernon, these mysterious people hounding him, the Poe Codec, his dad never being around, losing his mother and missing her, losing Lauren before he even had her—all of it. He was tired of the lies, the deception, the dishonesty he felt every time someone asked him what he was doing, as if it was something significant. Like it really mattered.

It was a riddle. A puzzle. A stupid game. Why the secrecy? So what if Vernon knew? If anybody knew? Brett's only concern was that it should end. He would not—could not—just quit. He knew the puzzle of Poe's hidden treasure would haunt him the rest of his life if he did. It had to be money. Lots of it. Why else would Poe go to all this trouble? Brett knew his reason for committing to the Poe Codec at the beginning was the thrill of the riddle, the challenge of problem-solving. But motives can change, and his did. The Poe Codec was no longer a problem—it was a solution to a problem. To his problems. He would finish this, take the money back to Indianapolis, divide it with Jordan and Lauren, and give the rest to his dad to pay off the medical debts from his mother's cancer. Maybe it would fix things. It *had* to fix things. It would finally be the end.

How would it end?

It was the same with movies, an obsessive/compulsive fault in him. Even if the movie was beyond idiotic, he watched it to its end. It was the same with books, almost as if he felt guilty for not finishing them, as if it was illegal to return a book to the library you didn't read all the way through or stop a movie halfway into it.

He couldn't quit on the Poe Codec.

No matter what.

He expected Vernon to say he could care less, but suddenly, for the first time in as long as Brett had known they were cousins, Vernon had no sarcastic, acerbic comments.

His only reply was "For real?"

"That's why I need your help, Vernon. You know the history of this town better than anyone else I know. I'm asking you. Look, I never thought I'd ever hear myself say this—but as a cousin—as maybe a *friend*—will you help me?"

Vernon only stood and stared at him.

"Look," Brett continued. "I just want it to be over. You can even have a share of the money, no matter how much we find. I'm so sick of this thing. I want it over."

"Are you serious? Why are you being so nice all of a sudden? I thought you couldn't stand me, and the only reason you come here every year is because my mom expects you."

"Well, that's pretty much true. But—have you ever been just flat-out tired?"

"Like how?"

"Like being tired of fighting things all the time. I don't know why I'm telling you any of this, but it's like my dad. I love him, at least I think I do, or I should, and I guess I know he loves me, but he's never around. I mean, when he is, he isn't, you know? When he *is* home, he's always on his computer working on something, or reading some book or journal, or on his phone. When I try to get him to do something, he always says he will later, but later never happens. I think sometimes I hate him, you know? Sometimes I wish he'd just leave for work one day and never come back. And that's my point, Vernon. I'm just tired of being mad at people all the time, you know? Like you, even. I'm sorry for how I treat you sometimes. Well, all these years, I guess."

Brett looked up at Vernon to see if he had even been listening, and to his amazement, he was.

Vernon was crying.

"What's wrong?" Brett asked, astounded to see Vernon expressing an emotion he had never witnessed from him before. Ever.

"My dad buys me stuff," Vernon said, too embarrassed to look into Brett's eyes.

"No kidding," Brett replied. "Great stuff."

"That's it," Vernon said. "That's all he does. I heard him tell my mom one night that sooner or later I'm going to have to man up and quit acting like a priss. He called me a priss, Brett! I'm not good at sports like Kyle, and I don't like doing a lot of stuff outside like he does. Dad knew I heard him, so he buys me stuff to make up for it. Do you know what it feels like to watch your dad play basketball with your brother when he's home while you hide behind the curtain inside and watch? I never get asked to play. I never get asked to do anything with them. I mean, Dad never even looks at me when he talks to me. I can't do stuff like Kyle does, Brett. Anything he does, he's great at. I suck at pretty much everything. I wish for once I could do something that would make dad proud of me."

Vernon began to sob, cutting off his own words. For the first time in his life, for as long as he had known Vernon was his cousin and was forced to tolerate him, Brett actually knew where Vernon was coming from, understood him, and as much as it made him cringe, he actually felt some kind of connection with him. Now Brett understood why he was the way he was. Only with Brett, it wasn't an older brother in college; it was his father. His father's work. Vernon's way of retaliating was to be the antithesis of his father's expectations, to be lazy, apathetic, obnoxious. At least Vernon had the spine to react openly. Brett just buried it, wilted, stuck his head in the sand and hoped his problems would fix themselves. Or disappear.

Nothing more than a coward.

He felt sorry for both of them. They were trying to survive the only way they knew how.

They really weren't so different after all.

What Brett's grandpa always used to tell him finally seemed to make sense: *No matter how bad you think you have it, someone else has it worse.*

Now he understood.

"So what's the first number again?" Vernon asked, smiling.

And Brett knew it was for real.

CHAPTER 7

"What does it say again?" Brett asked.

"Workingmen's Institute loom to analytical engine."

Brett had to admit that Vernon was amazingly adept at decoding the sequences, and even more skilled in understanding the application of the landmarks and items mentioned in the codes.

They had written the *Watchman's Chant* on a small sheet of notebook paper and numbered each letter, oblivious to the few people walking past and wondering why two boys were so fixated on a concrete etching that had been part of the town's landscape for over a hundred years.

```
A G A I N A D A Y I S
1 2 3 4 5 6 7 8 9 10 11

P A S T A N D A S T E P
12 13 14 15 16 17 18 19 20 21 22 23

M A D E N E A R E R T O
24 25 26 27 28 29 30 31 32 33 34 35

O U R E N D O U R T I M E
36 37 38 39 40 41 42 43 44 45 46 47 48

R U N S A W A Y A N D T H E
49 50 51 52 53 54 55 56 57 58 59 60 61 62

J O Y S O F H E A V E N
63 64 65 66 67 68 69 70 71 72 73 74

A R E O U R R E W A R D
75 76 77 78 79 80 81 82 83 84 85 86
```

Using the Poe Codec page with the multiple rows of numbers, they counted the letters each number indicated from the beginning of the chant, with fifty-four as *w*, thirty-five as *o*, and so on. The only complication was that there were no *k's, l's, or c's* in the chant, but Vernon easily determined these words without the missing letters.

54 35 31 4 5 2 24 22 28

11 10 40 14 15 46 21 37 45 29 36

42 47 60 64 30 74 71 56 60 46

57 77 74 2 46 58 82

WORINGMENS/INSTITUTE/OO

m/TO/ANAY TI/A/ENGINE

Workingmens Institute

Loom? to Analytical?

Engine

Analytical

"Loom? You mean like a weaving loom?" Brett asked. "Like the thing they used to make rugs and cloth and stuff?"

"Yeah, they've got one up on the second floor over there," Vernon said. "It's the town museum. They've got a bunch of stuff in there from the old settlements."

The Working Men's Institute was just a block over from the bench containing the chant. The large brick building was unique in that from the front, it resembled two separate buildings joined by a tall tower in the center, its many windows each arched in tannish-gray stone. Brett and Vernon passed the stubby World War I cannon next to the walkway leading to the entrance and ascended the steps to the large wooden doors. Above them, a gray stone arch with the letters and numbers *W.M.I 1838* and *1894* presented visitors with a sense of permanence, emphasized that the building not only contained history, but was historic itself.

"What's the deal with the analytical engine?" Brett asked.

"No idea. It'll probably have a plaque or sign by it."

They ascended the wooden stairway in the main vestibule, each step creaking, sending echoes throughout the open area. The main wall of the stairwell contained a near life-size painting titled *George Rapp Deeding the Present Site of New Harmony to Robert Owen*, where several figures stood or sat while this historic moment was captured on canvas. The boys reached the top of the staircase and walked to one of the two small wings containing artifacts from the community.

The loom was a gift from the Arthur Amsel estate, one of the larger exhibits in the museum from one of the oldest families in New Harmony. Size alone made it easy to locate. But trying to determine what Poe intended them to do with it was another entire mystery.

"So what are we looking for?" Vernon asked.

"I'm not sure. What does the plaque say?"

Vernon leaned over the blue-felt rope fencing in the exhibit to see the small sign providing details to the few visitors interested enough to observe what appeared to be little more than an antique weaving loom. "That's neat. It says this thing was automatic. You put a card with holes punched in it into the loom, and it would weave a design the card told it to. But I don't see anything about a code, or what it's got to do with an analytical engine, whatever that is."

Brett opened the pictures on his phone, quickly glancing around to see if they were being watched. He and Vernon were the only two on that floor of the museum.

He tapped on the file containing Poe's essay on Secret Writing. So far, every decoding system they had used was from the types detailed in Poe's essay. Brett remembered one of the methods Poe described involving the use of perforated cards. Held over a document, the holes in the card would allow letters to be exposed through the holes, resulting in the message being displayed.

"Vernon, get that card out of the loom."

"Sure. No problem," he replied, sarcastically.

"No, I'm serious. See if you can get it without getting caught."

"Are you insane? I can't just walk up to that thing and start pulling stuff off of it. I mean, usually I could care less what people think about me, but I really don't want to get a police record started before I get to high school, you know?"

"Yeah, but I think we need the card to find the next part of the code."

"You *think* you need it, or you *know* you need it?" Vernon asked.

"I'm pretty sure we need it."

"Great. So what's the big plan? Should I go get a black outfit and pull a pair of pantyhose over my head and lower myself from the ceiling so the receptionist downstairs won't see me—in broad daylight?"

"I don't want to steal it. I just want to borrow it for a few minutes."

"No way. If you need it so bad, why don't you get it?"

Good question. Brett knew it was a stupid idea, but so far, every part of the code, however implausible it appeared, seemed to work itself out. There had to be more.

"There's got to be a way to get in—"

Brett realized he had been talking to himself. Vernon had already walked back down the stairs to the guide sitting behind the small information desk near the entrance.

"Where'd you go?" Brett asked when Vernon returned several minutes later.

"Just asked the guide about the cards. She said there's a whole bunch of them on the table next to the loom. She said if we're careful, we can look at them."

"What did you tell her?"

"That we're doing research. I didn't lie."

Vernon was full of surprises.

"But there's more," Vernon smiled.

"What do you mean?"

"I asked her about the analytical engine thing. This is actually pretty cool. They've got one in the other wing upstairs."

"So, what is it?"

Vernon's eyes flashed as he talked, an excitement Brett had never experienced in him before.

"Margaret said that it's supposed to be the first ever computer."

"Who's Margaret?" Brett asked.

"She's the guide. Anyway, some guy named Charles Babbage made the plans for this machine that could do math. And guess how it works? She said with punch cards like the loom uses."

Brett began seeing the connections.

"Babbage drew blueprints for the machine, but he never built it.

Somebody here in New Harmony built one with this Babbage's plans a few years ago, but only a part of it. Margaret said it was because the thing was way too big to fit in here."

The analytical engine was only a part of Babbage's original plans (since the entire machine would have been enormous—far too impractical, as well as expensive, to actually have been built by a private engineer); only the "mill" or computation component was constructed. And even that was an enormous piece of machinery.

"So the deal is, we've got to use the card from the loom and put it in the machine to get the next clue. And both of the things we need are right here in the same building."

"Yep. Pretty good luck," Vernon said.

Brett was beginning to think that luck had nothing to do with it.

Or maybe everything.

CHAP73R 8

Brett was beginning to second-guess luck.

He and Vernon negotiated special permission to see the Analytical Engine under the guise of a personal research project. Which was true. Sort of. The museum curator, with Margaret's request, prepared the machine to power up, a chore that primarily required her plugging it in. The original schematics prescribed the gears to be driven by steam power, but electricity was the next best economical—and safest—form of contemporary power.

Brett placed the card from the loom into the designated slot, following the illustration on the informational plaque. He quickly noticed that the holes in all the display cards followed an identical pattern. (When Mr. Amsel donated the loom to the museum over a century and a half earlier, he also donated identical cards to ensure that any card used would provide the same results.)

The engine began to emit a series of rhythmic clicks, much like an old-fashioned key typewriter. A low whirring came from somewhere inside the metal interior.

From the far end of the machine, a thin slip of paper curled onto the small table attached to its side. Brett carefully held the paper in his hands, expecting to see more numbers or letters to lead them to the next code. But instead, he saw what resembled some sort of ancient cuneiform or some variation of hieroglyphics.

"Well, what do you think? Pretty impressive machine, isn't it? Did you see what you needed for your project?" the curator asked as she unplugged the electric motor. She appeared to be in her fifties, her small size allowing her to fit in many of the tighter spaces in the museum, and her permanent smile a sign that she truly loved her job—despite the lack of frequent visitors.

"Yeah, we wanted to see what actually made the output data," Vernon said. "It's amazing how similar the engine is to our computers. That Babbage guy was way ahead of his time."

One thing was sure about Vernon—he definitely could dial up the charm when he needed it.

"May we keep this little paper, to add to our research artifacts?" Brett asked the curator.

"Sure, no problem. Best of luck with your project," she said.

"Thanks," they both said, quickly turning towards the stairway.

A few moments later, Brett sat on the bench in the small park fronting the museum and stared at the slip of paper.

"What in the world is this?" he said, handing the paper to Vernon.

Vernon held it in his hands and shrugged his shoulders.

"Beats me. I have no—wait." He brought the slip closer to his face. "I've seen this before."

"You have?"

"Well, not this exact paper," he said, "but these marks. I know I've seen them somewhere."

Vernon stretched his body face-down across the bench with his hands behind his head. It was his favorite position to think. If it worked, Brett had no concern for how ridiculous it looked.

"I remember!" Vernon exclaimed after only a few seconds with his face directly where people actually sat. "Mr. Brumsfield's funeral!

Mr. Brumsfield was our neighbor, and he was really big into the Masons. When we went out to the cemetery, some of the older graves which had the compass and ruler Mason symbol on them also had that cuneiform-looking writing."

"Cuneiform?" Brett asked.

"Yeah, you know, that kind of writing we learned about in World History in seventh grade. You guys did learn about that at your school, didn't you?"

"Oh, yeah. I forgot," Brett lied.

"I asked someone what it was—I can't remember who—and they said it was Masonic code. They wouldn't tell me anything else."

Brett took his phone from his pocket and opened his search browser. He hoped he had enough charge left on his battery and enough cell reception to get online. He typed in *Masonic code*. One of the first results was *pigpen cipher*.

"What's it say?" Vernon asked.

"It says the pigpen cipher is what the Masons used when they wanted to write something in code. They made a tick-tack-toe-looking grid and wrote the letters *a* through *i* in it. Then in another grid, they wrote *j* through *r*, only they put little dots in different parts of the grid. Then they made two *x*'s and wrote *s* through *v* and *w* through *z*. So the shape of the box the letter was in was what they used as the code. All they had to do was move the letters around in the boxes, and as long as the other person had the same key, it would be really easy to figure out."

Brett opened an image containing an example of the pigpen cipher.

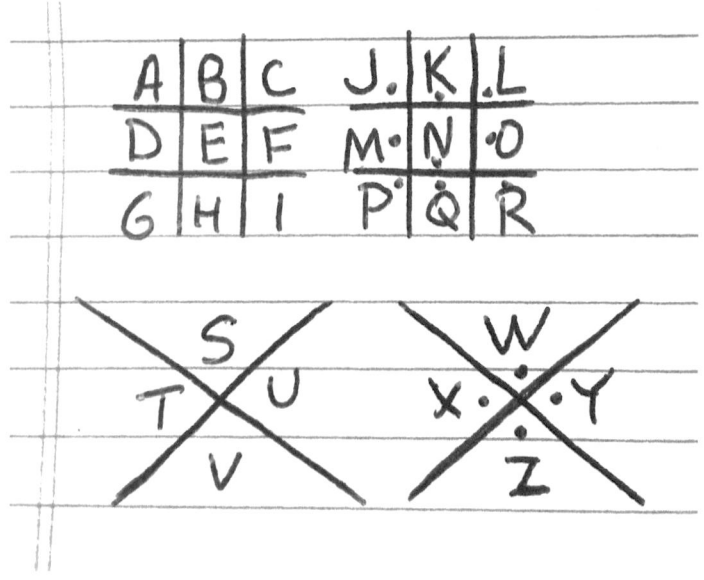

"Hold your phone next to the slip of paper, and I'll try to write down what the marks mean," Vernon said. "Hopefully, this one is the right code."

Vernon quickly cross-referenced the pigpen code with the symbols on the paper slip and wrote the letters *granarynnwcellar* on the notebook page.

"It worked!" Brett said as Vernon plopped down next to him. "The card from the loom worked in the engine. How did Poe know about the analytical engine? He died in 1849 and the engine wasn't designed until—"

"Eighteen-thirty-three," Vernon interrupted. "You're thinking about when that *Babbage guy* died, in 1871. You didn't read the rest of the plaque, did you?"

"No, why?"

"It said that Babbage was really interested in cryptography and that he broke something called the auto key code, which was supposed to be unbreakable. It said he even helped create codes for the English military."

"So if he was really into codes, and Poe was—"

"They probably knew each other, or at least knew about each other," Vernon said with an enthusiasm that drove Brett to question who it really was sitting next to him.

"So then Poe used a card meant for an automatic loom to make a code for a machine that hadn't been built yet. Man, I wish Lauren was here. This would blow her mind."

"We can probably get in if it's open." Vernon said.

"Where?"

"The Granary. In the cellar."

"The what?"

"The Granary. It's what the code is talking about."

"So what is it?"

"Just another old building around here."

"So can just anybody go in it?"

"No," Vernon replied. "But we will."

CHAP73R 9

Despite his tendency to repulse nearly everyone he knew nearly all of the time, Vernon did have a gift.

Getting into places he wasn't supposed to.

Brett smiled with new respect for him as Vernon turned the latch on the Granary cellar door.

The New Harmony Granary was one of the original buildings from Harmonie, the first settlement, a large four-story structure with a tall stone foundation supporting two floors of red brick, first used as a corn and flour mill. It had since been restored and refurbished to serve as a conference center and meeting hall.

"It's like a game," Vernon said. "It's not like there's a whole lot to do around here. We used to play hide-and-seek in the summers in elementary school, and this was the perfect place, because we weren't supposed to go down here, and everyone else thought it was haunted or something, so no one would find you. No one ever did find me."

Vernon wasn't boasting when he told Brett this. Brett could hear the tinge of regret over Vernon's words.

"So where should we go?" Vernon asked.

"I'm guessing north-northwest, if that is what the 'nnw' means in the directions. How in the world are we supposed to know which way that is down here?" Brett asked, frustrated that he hadn't had the foresight to bring a compass, since his phone was one of the older models without one.

"Check this out," Vernon said, holding his wrist to Brett's face. "My dad gave this to me last summer. They designed these watches for the Space Shuttle astronauts before they shut the program down, but the second hand on this one fell off, so they couldn't use it. They were going to throw it away until my dad asked if he could have it to give to me. Look. When you press this little button on the side, the hour and minute hands point to the north. See? So, if that way's north, then over here is north-northwest." As he pointed, he smacked his hand on the side of a large square pillar, the notches from being hand-hewn still protruding from its sides, one of the huge beams supporting the entire structure above them.

"Great," Brett said. "What in the world are we looking for? I don't see anything else here but this huge piece of wood. Do you think we're supposed to line it up with something, like in 'The Gold Bug'? Or maybe somehow get around it? Do you think whatever we're looking for is behind it?"

"Not behind it," Vernon replied. "In it."

CHAP73R 10

The voice laughed as the hand reached for the bank of light switches at the top of the stairs, just like in the clichéd horror movie when the suspense builds and the power suddenly cuts out. But the hand drew away from the wall. Why turn out the lights? There was nowhere to go. And why conceal it? Besides, the taser worked silently. All the hand would have to do is discharge a few bolts of electricity into one of them, knocking him unconscious, or perhaps merely incapacitating him, while the other, too terrified to speak or move, would gratefully comply.

The rest mere formalities.

The ears listened intently at the base of the stairs for any indication of success, for any suggestion that they had found it. The plan was crude, but it would be effective. It would work.

With little permanent damage.

Hopefully.

And then the treasure—or whatever it was—should be in the possession of someone deserving it, appreciating it. Sure, they were ingenious in breaking the codes, but they were children. They had yet to pay their dues to earn the pot of gold at the end of the rainbow. They were never forced to sit by, powerless, while their colleagues passed them on the promotional ladder, smirking behind their backs because they had yet to make any significant contribution to the field, had yet to write anything worthy of publication. They were immune to the torture of starting off strong, with years ahead of possibility, potential, only to find themselves halfway through, watching each dream fall from the branch, withered, every opportunity within their grasp passed along to someone with less experience, less intelligence, but more talk.

But finally, along came the opportunity of a lifetime, the opportunity to make a life. And this one was not going to slip away.

These two had no idea how critical this situation was.

It was life.

Or death.

For *all* of them.

The feet descended the steps, toe first, then the heel. Slowly. Cautiously. The voice chuckled once, laughing at itself. Why all the stealth, the secrecy? Maybe for the dramatic tension. Yet still, the feet continued their descent, each step more anxious than the previous one.

So close. So very close.

The head slid carefully around the entry, the body obscured by another of the large wooden beams. The eyes saw the boys tap on the suspiciously hollow-sounding beam and then lift a false-front section of the beam nearest them, revealing a hidden compartment. While Vernon held the panel, Brett lifted a metal box from the compartment.

The feet crept closer. The hand squeezed the rubber grip of the taser, the index finger lightly rubbing the curve of the trigger. The plastic was warm and moist in the hand, unaccustomed as it was to taking such drastic measures to obtain what the brain wanted.

But it was past the point of reconsideration.

The boys crouched over the box. Brett unlatched a clasp on the box's top, gently opening the lid. The eyes saw Vernon reach inside and remove a folded paper in one hand and a small silver object in the other.

It was true.

The hand reached out from behind Brett, the brain reasoning that if a struggle ensued, Vernon would be too terrified to interfere. With a quick flick of the trigger, the hand recoiled slightly as the two wires shot from the weapon and lodged themselves in the soft muscle between Brett's ribs. The finger squeezed intensely on the trigger, anticipating the sudden buzz and burst of electricity followed by Brett's short stifled scream.

But the taser only clicked.

Powerless.

Useless.

Suddenly, panic swam up the hand, the arm, the shoulder, the neck, and into the brain.

Some things seemed to never change.

CHAP73R 11

Brett screamed when the prongs of the taser wires penetrated his side. Instinctively, he swung his elbow backward to strike at the source of the searing pain. It struck something hard, then a muffled groan followed.

The body crumpled to the floor, its face hidden beneath an arm.

"Who are you?" Brett screamed, as the excruciating pain pierced his ribs and his elbow throbbed from the impact of the attack. "What's going on?"

The body lifted itself to its knees, holding its jaw. The fluorescent light overhead illuminated the features of the face, the cheek turning red.

As she stood all the way up, Brett and Jordan could see she was a woman, seemingly in her thirties, medium height and thin build, wearing gray yoga pants and a dark blue tank top, her dark hair pulled back into a pony tail. The light cast the right amount of shadow to accentuate her nose and high cheek bones, and in any other situation, Brett would have been fixated on her beauty.

She tossed the taser into the corner.

"Well, that was a waste of money," she said.

"What—what're you—" Brett was so furious, so frightened, the words stuck. He touched one of the taser probes protruding from his side, hesitant to pull them out from fear of how deeply they penetrated, and what held them in.

"It doesn't matter. Just let me have it," she said, calmly rubbing her jaw, "and I'm gone. I want the paper, too."

Brett knew her. He didn't know how, but he knew her.

"Come on. This is bad enough. Keep it from getting worse," she said.

"It's ours," Brett said, in tears. "We found it first."

"You mean *finders keepers, losers weepers*? Seriously, put the box and the paper on the floor and get away from it. I'll tell you how to get the probes out of your side, and I'll leave. For good."

Vernon sat on the floor next to the pillar, fear keeping him from moving.

Brett sensed hesitation in her voice. Even with one of them somewhat incapacitated, she could not control both of them, and Brett knew she deduced this shortly after the taser failed. She was reduced to merely talking them into giving her the box, threatening, bartering, whatever it took.

And Brett was not about to let that happen.

"Vernon, why don't you just hand me what you've got and go home. You've done your job," she said.

That voice. The face. *Where? When? How did he know her?*

"One more time, and that's it. Give it here."

"Why do you want it so bad? How do you even know what we've got?" Brett asked, stepping back a pace, the plastic taser shell scraping the floor as it followed the attached wires.

She laughed as she rubbed her warm cheek. "Okay, I've got a few minutes. I suppose you have a right to know. You remember when Tom sent the autograph samples to his friend Monique, the one from Purdue, so she could analyze them?"

"Yeah."

"Well, it's a pleasure to meet you," she said, bowing slightly. "He told me what you kids found, and I knew right away from the tests that it was something big. Really big. Huge. And it wasn't easy running the tests, considering I had to conduct them off campus, since Purdue wouldn't let me use their equipment. So I think I've earned my share."

"But—"

"I'm not finished. I asked Tom if he wanted in on it. You'll be happy to know he stuck up for you kids—at first. He said that he couldn't do something like that to his friend's kid, but when I told him what the letters alone would be worth, and that he'd get half, well, his mind sort of changed."

"You mean Dr. Laurence is a part of it?" Brett's mind reeled from the pain in his side and now the sudden struggle to process this new revelation. "Wait," he said, wincing as his arm bumped one of the probes. "You're the lady I saw the first day I was in town. You were jogging, and you said 'hi' to us. And you're the one who called me on my phone that night, right?"

"Let's see if I can get it right. 'And I would've gotten away with it if it weren't for you meddling kids,'" Monique said, putting her hands on her hips. "I used to love Scooby Doo."

"But how did you know—"

"About everything you were doing? Oh, sweetheart, it was easy. Technology is magic, isn't it, Vernon?"

"What?" Vernon asked, surprised to be suddenly thrust into the conversation. "Why are you asking me?"

"Oh, come on, Vernon. Don't pretend you don't know what I'm talking about," she said.

"I don't know," he replied defiantly.

"Vernon. I'm ashamed of you. You don't make a very good liar. Well, I guess you've just lost your share."

"What's she talking about, Vernon?"

"Oh, calm down, Brett," she said. "It's not that big of a deal. When you left the algebra book at the lab, I had Tom slip this really neat little GPS audio sensor inside the spine. It's about the size of the dot on an *i*. Everything the three of you said, I heard. Well, at least most of it. That's why I wanted the notes. But all I had to do was follow your directions right down here to this beautiful utopia."

"You heard everything we said?" Brett asked.

"Pretty much. Hopefully, they'll make one of those little sensors with video one day. And by the way, I think you *did* blow it with Lauren. After that little meltdown, the one you had before you left? Well, when you threw the book, it damaged the chip. I was hoping to get to hear how it was going to end, but I've got a pretty good guess. Too bad. She sounded like she really liked you. But I guess if all else fails, at least you can tell her it was all true, and you even got to hold it in your hand. Or at least Vernon got to."

"So what's Vernon got to do with all this?" he asked, terrified to hear the truth.

"Well, Vernon here helped me track you. He put a GPS tag inside your shoe, so all I had to do was follow the little red dot on my phone right to you. Thanks, Vernie. You're a real sweetheart."

"You liar! She's lying, Brett! She's trying to make you not trust me. I swear, I've never seen her before now. You know I know everybody in town. Check your shoe, Brett. Check it! See if there's anything in it."

"What? In my shoe?"

"Check it! You check your shoe, Brett, or I swear I'll rip your foot off and do it myself!"

Brett had never witnessed this violent side of Vernon before.

"It's okay, Vernon. I believe you," Brett said, pulling the wires from his side, wincing as he rubbed the two puncture holes left from the probes. "Don't worry. Look, Monique, or whatever your name really is, this huge treasure we've both been wanting? Here, take a look at it."

Brett took the object from Vernon's hand and held it in front of him, yet still out of her reach. It was a small silver locket, the kind that opened to reveal a miniature picture. He pushed the small latch on its side and opened it. Inside, a small painted picture of a dark-haired woman with thin lips smiled faintly within the oval, much like DaVinci's *Mona Lisa*.

"It's true," she whispered. "Poe's locket from his mother. The one she gave him before she died. Is the inscription inside?"

"What?" Brett said, refusing to accept her sudden politeness and assumed reverence.

"Does it say *'To my little Raven'*?"

"How did you know that?" Vernon asked.

"Vernie. I've spent nearly every minute of spare time my entire life figuring out all I can about Poe. It's already cost me a marriage, and it's almost costing me another, but this locket—this locket is worth all of it. Poe was supposed to have worn it around his neck all his life. No one ever saw the inside, but the legend is that his mother had it inscribed before she died."

Brett examined the piece of metal cupped in his hand. So this was it? The end? All that work, all he lost—Jordan, Lauren, all of it for *this*? He felt cheated, used, like Edgar Allan Poe personally defrauded him. He felt stupidly naive, playing along with the game, spending the millions over and over again in his daydreams. Seeing the look on his father's face when he gave him the money to clear the debts. Getting to deliver Jordan's and Lauren's share and telling them the whole story, that leaving them behind was the only way he knew to protect them. All the sacrifice. All the danger. For nothing. Other than knowing that all this really did lead to something. Just not what he expected. Or would even get to keep.

Nothing more than a dream with a bad ending.

Yet a woman stood before him nearly deranged with excitement at finding it. The Poe Codec was amusing, Brett fully admitted it, and he was relieved to see that it actually did have an end, but the finale was nothing he'd expected. And far from what he wanted. His reward for solving the Poe Codec? Two small puncture wounds in his side, two former friends who would refuse to ever acknowledge his existence again, a relationship with a girl that would never happen.

And no way out.

But maybe there was.

And suddenly, everything became clear.

If this woman wants this trinket, it's hers. Give it to her, she disappears, he returns home and confesses it all to Lauren and Jordan, that he deliberately cut his ties with them to protect them. Be the protector. Then he would concoct an excuse for not going to the University to avoid confronting Dr. Laurence. Be the coward. Bury it all and move forward. And life returns to normal.

Whatever normal is. Or was.

But his planning abruptly fizzled when Monique reached behind her, and as her hand moved forward, it held a piece of chrome.

A pistol.

And planning suddenly became ludicrous.

"Give them to me. I'm not asking again."

Brett was through with the hero role. This was not a movie where the gun is empty or the round jams in the chamber, granting the hero enough time to land a punch or a roundhouse kick to the antagonist's hand, dislodging the gun safely out of reach. No diving for the weapon as it slides across the floor, no grabbing it at the last possible moment, holding the antagonist in custody until the police arrive. The gun was real. The dilemma was real.

And it was over.

"Here," was all Brett could say, simply placing the locket and papers on the floor and backing away, his hands and arms beginning to shake, his chest beginning to tighten as his brain began fully processing the events transpiring in the last few seconds.

Brett had never seen the inside of a gun barrel. In his daydreams, he played the protector, the one staring down danger, fighting it into submission. Now, all he could do was stand.

And shiver.

And fight his tears.

"You chose wisely, Brett," Monique said as she knelt to take the items.

The gun was pointing to the floor, but it would have mattered little. She could have tossed the gun to the top of the stairs and Brett and Vernon—standing against the wall like granite sculptures— would not have moved a muscle, would not have been *able* to move.

"Keep the box," she said, carefully placing the papers and locket in a small plastic case and then into her backpack. "You can show Lauren and Jordan that it was real after all. They might give you another chance. You never know. I hate that it had to end this way. I really hoped it would be different. Adieu."

Monique backed towards the stairwell and disappeared up the steps.

Vernon could not stop shaking.

Brett could not stop crying.

PART III:
BACK TO THE
BEGINNING

CHAPTER 1

Three days later, Brett shoved the lead box beneath his own bed, back home in Indianapolis. His visit to New Harmony over for another year, and the drive home with his father just as wordless as always.

Home. He never envisioned loving a place he hated so much. But things changed. He and Vernon agreed not to report the Granary incident to the police, although both were unsure of their reasons. Fear of an investigation drawing public attention — if only briefly — the notoriety eliciting a perpetual fear of Monique returning? Depression from his alienation of nearly everyone Brett loved? Perhaps he was exhausted. Physically. Mentally. Emotionally.

Perhaps enough was enough.

He assumed that if he and Vernon did report Monique's theft of the locket, they would be required to produce evidence, and all he had was an empty lead box approximately the size of a thick hardback book and two small punctures in his side scabbing over. Still, even if Monique could be found and prosecuted, her only crime was theft of old papers and a small piece of junk jewelry — if *theft* was the right term, since the items actually did not belong to her *or* Brett . He knew Vernon would testify that she did have a gun, but could they prove the gun was loaded?—which in Indiana is the difference between a misdemeanor or a felony, a legal detail Brett had already researched on his phone during the drive home.

Besides, it was only a locket and old papers. No money, no treasure, nothing of significant value. The box's uniqueness might have some worth to a specialty collector, but if it did, Monique certainly would have taken it.

Brett's main regret was that he wished he could have read the letter.

But it was true. All of it. Edgar Allan Poe really did hide something in New Harmony, Indiana. He really did try to deceive Rufus Griswold as retribution for attempting to destroy Poe's reputation. But it was just a locket. Poe kept referring to it as a *treasure* . . .

Then Brett understood. It *was* a treasure. *To Poe.* The woman's picture. It had to have been his wife Virginia or his mother. Even in Poe's time, it may have been worth only a few dollars. But now . . .

So Monique knew after all. She knew exactly what it was and the value it might have on the current collectibles market—if she planned to sell it.

But he had the box, proof that the Poe Codec was real. Brett had no deep-seated sense of accomplishment, of winning, what he thought he would feel after it was over, the emotion he thought he was chasing all along. But his reaction was not about losing the locket. It was more. Much more. He lost respect for Dr. Laurence, who betrayed him, a family friend, someone he admired. One of the last people he would ever expect to deceive him. He lost a big piece of his summer vacation, the summer before high school. He lost his best friend, someone who would forget, but might never forgive. He lost any hope with Lauren.

He was tired of losing.

Maybe that's what you find when you fail to search for what truly matters.

He still loved Jordan and Lauren, loved them both, and that was why he was giving them the box. Not as the clichéd peace offering but to prove that it all *was* real, nothing more. The Poe Codec had cost him more than he ever dreamed.

And he loathed it.

He understood how Frodo felt carrying the Ring in *The Lord of the Rings*.

Brett held his phone and typed a simple text message: *I have something you two might want. Come by my house if you can . . . I'm sorry . . .*

CHAPTER 2

"So what do you want?" Jordan asked, standing next to Lauren on Brett's front porch, her eyes forcing Brett to avert his own.

"First of all, I—you guys want to come in?" Brett asked as pleasantly as he could, acutely sensing their animosity toward him.

"Look, I've got stuff to do, so hurry up," Jordan said, walking past Brett into the living room, displaying no mercy, no grace. Lauren followed.

"You guys want something to drink?"

"Just tell us what's so important so we can get out of here," Jordan replied.

Brett hoped with everything in him that Lauren would come to his defense, would tell him everything was okay, that things could be the way they were. But all she did was stare at the chair next to her.

Brett took a deep breath.

And told them everything. The rest of the Poe Codec. Who was sending the emails, making the phone calls, how Monique took the locket, about the taser. About the gun. About why he did what he did. He poured it all out. All of it. If rebuilding their relationship was impossible, they would at least know the truth. As Brett told the story, Jordan never flinched, not a single hairline crack in his veneer of disdain. He just leaned against the wall, his arms folded, staring at Brett as he spoke.

Silence followed Brett's narrative. Then Lauren looked at him and smiled, her eyes reflecting the light from the window. He almost cried, she was so beautiful. She walked towards him. Given all that had happened, he had expected her to shove him, slap him, kick him, or just turn her back to him.

Instead, she took his hand.

Her hand was soft, warm. She looked into his eyes for what seemed like forever, touched her top lip lightly with her tongue, and kissed him. One kiss, lip-to-lip, soft, but with meaning, not a friendship kiss.

Much more.

Brett couldn't move, couldn't speak.

Neither could Jordan.

CHAPTER 3

The silence roared.

No one knew what to say, what to do. All three were shocked at what just occurred.

Then Jordan interpreted the kiss's connotation. He was now on his own. Lauren evidently dissented from his condemnation of Brett. He was the third wheel. Odd man out. The sixth player on the basketball court. Every left-out cliché he could remember drifted across Jordan's mind.

It wasn't fair.

Brett said he was protecting them. From what? From a psychotic woman with a gun?

A gun . . .

Brett had actually looked into a gun barrel pointed at his face. Not a plastic toy like the ones they played with endlessly when they were younger, but a real firearm aimed at him. Ready to fire. Ready to hurt him.

Mortally.

"Well, it still isn't fair," was all Jordan could respond, breaking the awkward silence still hovering in the room, still unwilling to admit that he could forgive Brett, that he could not hold the grudge against him, that Brett did what he himself could never do.

"So what are you wanting to show us?" Jordan asked.

"Not show you. Give you. A souvenir from New Harmony."

Brett reached under the couch and placed the box on the table.

The dull gray top and sides looked like an artifact from a medieval castle, completely out of context on the glass tabletop.

"The box?" Lauren asked. "You kept it?"

"Yeah, but that's all. She took the locket."

"It doesn't matter, because it's all true. It wasn't a hoax," Lauren replied.

"It's yours. Both of you. I don't know how you're going to figure out how to divide it up, but I don't want it. The thing's sort of cursed, you know? At least I think so."

He slid the box across the table to Jordan, who lifted the lid. It was over. It was all real.

And now it was worth it.

"That's cool," Jordan said, peering inside the box.

"What? The cat etched on the bottom?" Brett asked.

"Yeah. I guess that was sort of like Poe's trademark or something, you think?" Jordan replied.

"Yeah. If it's a black cat. Bad luck."

"Let me see," Lauren said, reaching across the table and pulling the box to her. She carefully picked the box up and turned it over, turned it on its side, looked intently at it from every angle she could position it in, careful not to drop its weight on the table top.

"What are you doing?" Jordan asked.

"There's more," she said.

"More what?" Brett asked.

"Remember Poe's story 'The Black Cat'?"

"No," Jordan replied.

"I remember Mrs. Savelle talking about it a little," Brett said.

"There's no way," Lauren said. "It can't be that simple."

"What?" Brett asked.

"In the story, the narrator kills his wife and bricks her up inside a wall in the basement. The only way the cops find the body is when they hear a cat screaming inside the wall. A black cat leads them to the body! We've got to get this box open!"

"How much more open can we get it?" Jordan asked. "If you haven't noticed, the thing's empty."

"Do you have a screwdriver or something?" Lauren asked.

"For what?" Jordan asked.

"To try to pry the sides open. I don't want to mess it up if we don't have to."

CHAPTER 4

The three stood over the box as it rested on the workbench in Brett's garage, the boys leery of Lauren's intentions. Brett held the hammer, knowing what they did to the box would be permanent. The screwdriver only bent the joints tighter together. They had no choice. Intact, the box might still have monetary value, nothing significant, but perhaps as an historical artifact. Breaking it open would be comparable to using the back of Abraham Lincoln's original draft of the Gettysburg Address as scratch paper for math homework. Unthinkable.

But the question would perpetually haunt them if they failed to find out. Was there more? Did the cat really mean what Lauren theorized? The unknown. Curiosity. The very element that drew them into this odyssey from the beginning, what still drove them further on. In every instance, it was one more code, one more clue, one more direction, one more location, place. And here again.

One more.

Brett turned the box on its side, breathed deeply, raised the hammer and struck along the inside edge of the box. The sides and bottom were joined in a fashion similar to a wooden drawer, what Brett knew from industrial technology class as dovetail joints. He assumed that if lead reacted the same as wood, the pieces would easily break apart at the joints.

They did.

And then they saw it.

The false bottom.

With the lid open, the surface etched with the cat image appeared to be the actual bottom, but it was really a piece perfectly fitted above the true bottom, leaving about three quarters of an inch between the two lead pieces.

Just enough.

"What's in it?" Jordan asked, nudging over Brett's shoulder.

"Some papers," he replied.

"No. I'm done," said Jordan. "No more. I'm not going through anymore of this."

"Wait. Lauren, here," Brett said, stepping away from the bench.

Lauren reached inside. One document was tri-folded, a letter, while the others were bound by a strand of black ribbon. She opened the letter and read the contents aloud.

To Whomever holds this in his hands–

I trust that you are not Mr. Griswold. If you are, my humblest apologies, for I confess that you are of a much higher genius than I've given you credit. But the Rufus Griswold I know would have ended his journey after obtaining what he thought was his prize, seeing no earthly value to it save what he could gain by its sale. But who would buy dreams?

I will lean on intuition that you are not the man I name. Thus, I must congratulate you on your persistence to see your odyssey to its end. Remember in the beginning I informed you that "I entombed this fruit of my life's work in a safe location near my destination." I have led you to believe that you would find a treasure at the end of your quest, a prize worthy of the challenge. You undoubtedly found the box and the locket within. This was for Mr. Griswold's sake. The letter you found, addressed to him, told him of the actual value of the locket, that it was in fact a copy of the one my beloved mother Eliza gave me shortly before her passing, a very inexpensive one, I can assure you, as the locket my dear mother imparted to me had an etching inside, as well, but with the word 'forevermore' encoded in the Masonic code, or more commonly, the pigpen cipher. I took the measure of giving him the letter to ensure that if he did choose to pursue this folly, he would find his venture ill-gained, and that he would detest me even all the more upon my demise, and that his quest would end with an empty trophy and many exhausted resources. I trusted that he would know little of my works, my true art, and that the subtleties fixed therein would go quite unnoticed.

But you, reader, you are the wiser! You knew the significance of the Black Cat! You are to be praised, for you understand the work of genius. Those around me know little of what I do, or what I say. They do not understand, nor do they endeavor to do so. But in the ancients' words–'Victor pergit ad spolia'–'to the victor, go the spoils.'

You will find with this document the true prize. It is often understood that great art is truly appreciated only after the death of the artist. Such I feel is my fate.

You hold in your hands a copy–from my own hand–of the poem that made my name spoken among the many. For dire need of medicine and fuel for warmth for my beloved Virginia, I exchanged the work for fourteen dollars, a pittance of its true value, which of course no earthly currency can equal. I trust that if you have studied my work well enough to have solved the clues to this quest, you will realize the value of what I now give you.

It is customary that copies of works of art hold more value when penned in the maker's own hand, especially those progressions of the art–the drafts, the revisions, the alterations. This holds true especially post-mortem. I trust the same in your time, be it ten or ten score and ten years.

A copy of <u>The Raven</u> is enclosed with my first drafts of <u>The Tell-Tale Heart</u>, <u>The Cask of Amontillado</u>, <u>The Pit and the Pendulum</u>, <u>Black Cat</u> and <u>Annabelle Lee</u>. Only ink scribbles now, but perhaps a king's ransom then.

I am, Respectfully,

E. A. Poe

EPILOGUE

Article in the Indianapolis Sun

Poe Documents the 'Real Deal'

Associated Press—Researchers from the United States Library of Congress and the National Archives have concluded that the documents recently discovered and supposedly written by Edgar Allan Poe, the nineteenth century author most famous for his poem 'The Raven," are authentic. Submitted last month by Ellen Savelle, an Indianapolis, Indiana schoolteacher, on behalf of an anonymous party, the documents comprise a small collection of Poe's original drafts of his major works, including a hand-written letter.

Suspicions about how Savelle acquired the documents prompted a federal investigation, which determined that the collection was obtained legally, and that "all parties involved in the exchange were well within the legal constraints in this acquisition," said Chief Investigator Danielle Lansberry.

After the Library of Congress processes the documents in digital format for archival purposes, Savelle has been authorized to transfer their ownership to the University of Virginia's Edgar Allan Poe archive, with one of the manuscripts to be presented on loan to the Edgar Allan Poe Museum in Richmond, Virginia, in accordance with the instructions of the anonymous party.

"It is impossible to overstate the historical and literary significance of these documents," said John Reynolds, Curator of the University of Virginia's Poe Collection. "We are extremely grateful and indebted to Ms. Savelle and the private donors, especially considering the value of such artifacts."

A spokesperson from the Poe Museum stated that the donated manuscript would be "the most significant donation since the acquisition of Poe's locket." (An anonymous descendant of the Poe family gifted the small locket to the museum in 2008. It attracted little media attention until it was authenticated as the one Poe was thought to have worn around his neck his entire life. The locket contained a small miniature portrait of his mother Eliza Poe and the word "forevermore" etched on the inside cover in the Masonic or "pigpen" cipher, leading experts to verify its authenticity.)

According to Savelle, the group did accept an undisclosed amount from the sale of the "Black Cat" manuscript, but declined to offer the other manuscripts for sale at auction. "They feel documents of this importance have been hidden for too long, and they belong to the world," she said. "Now the world can see Poe in the process of creating his art."

The documents are rough drafts of Poe's most popular short stories and a poem: "The Tell-Tale Heart," "The Cask of Amontillado," "The Pit and the Pendulum," and "Annabelle Lee." Scholars plan to study the proofreading and revision marks made by Poe in an attempt to better understand his writing process.

THE POE CODEC

Article in the Friedman University School Newspaper, *The Dog Tag*

Dr. Thomas Laurence, renowned Chemistry professor and expert in thin-layer chromatography, resigned abruptly from his position at the University this past week, leaving the Department of Chemistry scrambling to fill his position before the coming Fall semester. University officials declined to provide specific details pertaining to his sudden resignation, other than stating that it was "for personal reasons."

Students enrolled in summer courses under Dr. Laurence should report to class as normal.

Article in *New Harmony Living*

New Harmony resident Vernon Trimble, 16 years old, recently published his first novel, *The Poe Codec*, inspired by the events surrounding the discovery of Edgar Allan Poe's original drafts of some of his most famous works two years ago.

Written for a young adult audience, *The Poe Codec* is a suspense-treasure hunt that fictionalizes the method by which Poe's documents were found. The two main characters, Brett and Jordan, with the help of their friend Lauren, try to decode clues Poe supposedly left for his nemesis, Rufus Griswold, leading to a hidden treasure. Breaking the code for each clue proves difficult enough, but the characters must stay one step ahead of an unknown individual after the same prize.

Vernon says he chose to make the novel as personal as possible.

"I used my cousin's name as one of the main characters because I thought it'd be cool for him to read about himself in a book. I guess I used my name for the same reason," Vernon says, smiling.

He chose his hometown of New Harmony as the final setting because of the rich historical heritage of the utopian community.

"It just made sense. Edgar Allan Poe would have fit in perfectly in our town. Plus, there's some really neat places that add a lot to the mystery."

When asked about where he got his ideas for the details of the novel, beyond the popular headline news story, Vernon only smiles and says, "It's sort of like being a magician. You can't reveal the secrets to your tricks, because if you do, where's the magic?"

Vernon is unsure if he intends to write a sequel to *The Poe Codec*, or if he even intends to continue writing at all.

"I don't know if I'm cut out to be a writer for a career. It was easy to write this one because I followed the real story in the news so close. I guess maybe I could write about what happens to the characters after the story, but that might end up being boring," he says.

The Poe Codec, written by Vernon Trimble, one of New Harmony's own, can be purchased at all major bookstores and is available for electronic download.

MICHAEL CRANDELL

Classified Advertisement in the *Playa del Carmen Courier* — Mexico
(as translated)

For Sale: Antique locket with painted miniature inside. In good condition. Must sell. Asking $50.00 or best offer. Call (282) 908-9876. Ask for Monique.

ACKNOWLEDGEMENTS

This is the part of the book that most of us skip over to get to the reason why we chose to read this book to begin with, since this part usually only contains heartfelt recognition of people important to the author, people who helped make this thing you're holding in your hands more than just a neat idea, people unknown and irrelevant to us. But that's okay.

Usually the most important parts of something are what we *can't* see.

Special recognition goes to:

Mrs. Kathy Riordan, my good friend and former language arts teaching colleague, for her ceaseless insistence that I pursue publication of this manuscript, and for her continual encouragement when I was content with it being just a lesson in narrative writing.

Mr. David Bunner, my uncle-in-law, for his legal guidance—pro bono.

Mr. David Purvis, my friend, my colleague, my brother. The epitome of what constitutes a friend. My spotter—inside the gym, but even more so outside. One of those rare individuals who inspires people around them to seek *arête*.

Stephanie, Jordan, Lauren, for making our home always the place we want to be when we're somewhere else, and quite simply, for being the reason why I do what I do.

ABOUT THE AUTHOR

Michael Crandell, a middle and high school English teacher for over twenty years, holds a Bachelor of Science degree in English and a Master of Secondary Education, both from the University of Southern Indiana. He lives with his wife Stephanie, his son Jordan, and his daughter Lauren in southwestern Indiana.

The Poe Codec is his first novel.

www.ingramcontent.com/pod-product-compliance
Lightning Source LLC
Chambersburg PA
CBHW050942120626
46552CB00001B/330